"I had a good time tonight," Travis said.

"Me, too." *Great, in fact.* Savannah headed for the porch before she did something crazy like invite him to spend the night, and not on her couch this time. She already had too much on her mind. She didn't need to add a serious relationship to the mix.

"Savannah?"

She turned and watched him walk slowly toward her, still looking too good to be true in the dim light. "Yeah?"

"You going to let me take you out again sometime?"

"Maybe." Damn if her voice didn't crack a little.

The wooden steps creaked as he climbed one then two, putting himself eye to eye with her. "I guess that's better than a no."

She smiled a little and realized her butterflies had returned with a vengeance. She started to turn away, but a voice inside her head screamed at her to not let him go. Not allowing the time to talk herself out of it, Savannah reached up and framed Travis's face with her palms, heart racing as she looked up at him and gently drew him closer.

Dear Reader,

I hope you're enjoying the story of the Baron family that was launched last month with Donna Alward's *The Texan's Baby.* I was happy to be able to write the story of another Baron sister, Savannah, who has left full-time barrel racing to put her efforts into her new passion, the farm store on her family's Texas ranch. But when a health scare prompts her to begin searching for the mom who abandoned her, she doesn't expect that search to bring her face-to-face with the love of her life. Private investigator Travis Shepard doesn't expect love again after the loss of his first wife, but life has a funny way of throwing unexpected things—and people—into our paths.

We all fear loss, but it's unfortunately a part of life. One of the biggest challenges we can face is finding the courage to love again after one of these losses. That's what Savannah and Travis have to do to find their happily ever after. I hope you enjoy their journey.

And be sure not to miss *The Texan's Little Secret* by Barbara White Daille next month. It's the story of the third Baron sister, Carly, a big secret and a second chance at love. The Baron siblings' stories will continue in the months following when talented authors Pamela Britton, Cathy McDavid and Tanya Michaels bring you more wonderful romances for the three Baron brothers.

Trish Milburn

THE TEXAN'S
COWGIRL BRIDE

———

TRISH MILBURN

HARLEQUIN® AMERICAN ROMANCE®

Special thanks and acknowledgment are given to Trish Milburn for her contribution to the Texas Rodeo Barons continuity.

Recycling programs
for this product may
not exist in your area.

ISBN-13: 978-0-373-75527-1

THE TEXAN'S COWGIRL BRIDE

Copyright © 2014 by Harlequin Books S.A.

Printed in U.S.A.

www.Harlequin.com

ABOUT THE AUTHOR

Trish Milburn writes contemporary romance for the Harlequin American Romance line and paranormal romance for the Harlequin Nocturne series. She's a two-time Golden Heart Award winner, a fan of walks in the woods and road trips, and a big geek girl, including being a dedicated Whovian and Browncoat. And from her earliest memories, she's been a fan of Westerns, be they historical or contemporary. There's nothing quite like a cowboy hero.

Books by Trish Milburn

HARLEQUIN AMERICAN ROMANCE

1228—A FIREFIGHTER IN THE FAMILY
1260—HER VERY OWN FAMILY
1300—THE FAMILY MAN
1326—ELLY: COWGIRL BRIDE
1386—THE COWBOY'S SECRET SON*
1396—COWBOY TO THE RESCUE*
1403—THE COWBOY SHERIFF*
1450—HER PERFECT COWBOY**
1468—HAVING THE COWBOY'S BABY**
1482—MARRYING THE COWBOY**

*The Teagues of Texas
**Blue Falls, Texas

To everyone who has suffered the loss of someone they loved with all their heart and found the courage to love again.

Chapter One

Savannah Baron hit Send on the online order form for more canning jars and scratched another item off her to-do list. She grabbed the separate list she'd made for Gina Shelton, her employee, and walked out of her small office into the kitchen area of the Peach Pit, the farm store she managed on her family's large north Texas ranching and farming operation. She walked up next to where Gina was sliding a fresh batch of fried peach pies into the glass-fronted display counter next to the cash register.

"Ben and Juan will be in later with a few more bushels of peaches. Half of them are for fresh baskets, half for a new batch of preserves. Ingrid Tollemey will be by around four this afternoon to pick up the dozen pies for the church fair. And—"

Gina smiled and held up her hand. "You're only going to be gone a couple of days, not a month."

Savannah nodded, realizing she was micromanaging. She hated when she did that. "And you've done this before. Sorry. I get carried away."

"It's okay. But you better get going."

Savannah looked at the clock and hurried back into her office to grab her keys. She was supposed to meet her friend and fellow barrel racer Abby Morgan in Mineral Wells in three hours for a weekend of rodeo. It was about a hundred-mile drive, but she still had to load Blue-bell into the horse trailer and toss her luggage and gear into the truck.

She heard the front door open, but she let Gina take care of the new customer. But when the phone rang, Savannah blew out a breath and answered.

"Peach Pit. How can I help you?"

"Savannah, I need for you to come to the house," her father said. "I've been going over the financials for your little store, and I have some concerns."

"Now's not a good time, Dad." Not that anytime was going to be particularly good.

Since her dad had broken his leg during a senior rodeo and been laid up at home, he'd been driving everyone bonkers with his pronouncements about how they should all be doing their jobs differently, which meant the way he would do them. She'd bet good money he was even pointing out ways Anna, the family's longtime housekeeper, could more efficiently vacuum or wash the dishes. If Savannah found a genie in a bottle who said he'd grant her only one wish, it would be to instantly heal her dad. Then he could go back to work at the Baron Energies company headquarters in Dallas or focus on anything other than her slice of the Baron pie.

"You can spare a few minutes. This won't take long."

The way he said it made her stomach knot. That didn't sound good, not good at all.

"Just close up or leave that girl who works for you in charge."

Savannah pressed her fingertips against the building ache in the middle of her forehead. "Gina, Dad. Her name is Gina. And I can't come now. I'm about to load up and head to Mineral Wells."

"It's Friday already? Damn, weeks are getting shorter."

No, he was just growing older and absolutely refusing to acknowledge it or slow down. That's what had gotten him that nasty broken leg, thinking he could still rodeo like he had forty years earlier.

"I'll see you when you get back," he said.

Though if she were lucky, by the time she returned from Mineral Wells he would have moved on to bugging someone else. She loved her dad dearly, but he was a man who liked to put his stamp on everything, especially things that had the name Baron attached to them in any way.

Before he could say anything else, she hung up and headed for the door, waving to Gina as she passed her. She had the craziest fear that if she didn't hurry, her dad would have someone roll him out in his wheelchair so he could talk business as she was loading up. And right now, she just wanted a weekend away to indulge her lifelong love of rodeo, hang out with a good friend and just maybe ogle a cute cowboy or two.

But ogling took a backseat to running barrels. She didn't ride as much as she used to, but it was still in her blood. The power of Bluebell beneath her, the thrill of cutting as close to the barrels as she could without tipping them over, the desire to win.

Besides, as busy as she stayed at the ranch, when would she find time to squeeze in a date? No, she'd had her time having fun with cowboys on the circuit. Now, she was a businesswoman determined to be as successful in her new endeavor as she'd been during the height of her racing years.

The warmth of the late-morning sun hit her as she stepped out of the store and headed for her truck. The drive up to the barns didn't take long, but it made her anxious nonetheless. She eyed the impressive stone-and-wood home where she'd grown up as she passed by, hoping her dad was already otherwise occupied.

She waved at Luke Nobel, the ranch manager, as she parked next to the barn. She hurried into the cooler interior, irrationally concerned that her dad would find a way of making her stay to discuss business. Now that he'd pretty much accepted that Lizzie, her older sister, was doing just fine temporarily filling his shoes at Baron Energies, her dad seemed to be searching for any way to assert that he was still the man in charge around the ranch, in their family.

A few minutes later as she guided Bluebell into the trailer, she finally began to relax a little. After all, if there was one thing her father loved as much as being a tough businessman, it was rodeo. Thus the broken leg.

She ran her hand down the sorrel mare's neck. "You ready to race?"

As if she understood, Bluebell tossed her head in a way that looked as if she were nodding. Savannah smiled as she closed the gate on the trailer and headed toward the driver's side of her truck. She'd ridden other horses in events before, but none had even come close to Bluebell's natural ability. The mare seemed to thrive on the competition every bit as much as Savannah did.

Savannah slid into the truck and started the engine. "Well, girl, let's show them how it's done."

As the miles ticked away, Savannah's mind wandered from the upcoming competition back to the farm store. She was putting her heart and soul into the Peach Pit, building its offerings and reputation. She had big plans for the store, if only her dad would stop nitpicking. He ought to just be glad she was home more than she used to be. But since breaking his leg in that rodeo for old coots wanting to relive their glory days, he'd questioned everything from how she arranged the store's products to the font on the sign.

If she were more like either of her sisters, she'd have told him to cut it out by now. But she wasn't. No, while she wasn't a pushover, she was the quietest of the three girls, the one who didn't tend to raise a fuss. She didn't like turmoil or contributing to it. There were already enough dynamic personalities in her family—her dad, Carly, her younger brother Jet— who were more than enough to fill that role of fuss-raiser. She just wanted to do her job, do it well, and enjoy time with her family, making up for all the time she'd spent on the road.

As the rodeo grounds finally came into view, she let those concerns fade away. She felt the familiar surge of excitement she always did on competition day. Sometimes she still missed traveling the circuit, but then she'd remember the times she'd been alone in some motel in Wyoming or California yearning for the comforting environs of her family's ranch. After years of living and breathing rodeo, she'd scaled back. Now she competed about once a month, devoting the rest of her time to the Peach Pit, making a name for the store and herself with her peach- and pecan-flavored treats. The Barons were driven, and she was no different in that respect.

She made the turn into the area that held the outdoor arena and the expo center and spotted Abby's rig. Since Abby was a full-time cowgirl with one national championship to her name and well on her way to another, she traveled with a nice horse trailer with living quarters. Sometimes her brother Aaron, a bareback and saddle bronc rider, would travel with her. This weekend, however, Aaron was home nursing a nasty case of the spring flu. So it was a girls' weekend, just what Savannah needed.

Savannah smiled as she pulled up behind Abby's trailer

to find her friend kicked back under the pullout shade with a big glass of lemonade.

"About time you got here, girlfriend," Abby said as Savannah slid from her truck.

"Some of us have other jobs, oh, lady of leisure."

Abby laughed and hopped up to give Savannah a hug. "Want some lemonade?"

"In a bit. Need to let Bluebell work out the kinks first."

Abby followed her to the back of Savannah's trailer. "You have a run on peach pies? That why you're late?"

Savannah glanced at her friend. "Just for that, you don't get any of the one I brought."

"Now that's just mean."

Savannah laughed, feeling more of her stress sliding away as she opened the trailer and got Bluebell out on solid ground. She led the mare away from the cluster of trucks and trailers, and Abby fell into step beside her.

"I just had to make sure I'd taken care of everything before I left for the weekend. And then Dad called as I was trying to get out the door."

"Still a thorn in your side?"

Savannah gave her friend an exasperated look. Abby had always thought the elder Baron should "take a chill pill."

"He's just frustrated because he can't go to work. He's bored."

"Brock Baron and boredom. That's a bad combo."

While Savannah had to agree, she also felt as if she had to defend her dad. He might drive them all crazy in turns, might be a trifle too demanding, but he was a good father. Sometimes you just had to look a little deeper to find it under all the gruff exterior.

"As soon as he's able to go back to work, things will get better."

"When will that be?"

"Don't know yet." Not soon enough. "A break like that isn't an easy thing at his age. To hear him tell it, the physical therapist is going to kill him first."

After Savannah tied up Bluebell next to Abby's blond mare, Rosie the Pivoter, she accepted a cold glass of lemonade and sank into the lawn chair next to Abby's. As soon as she was seated, she laughed.

"What?"

"I just realized why you parked here."

"I have no idea what you're talking about." But the mischievous look on her face said otherwise.

Savannah snorted. "So you didn't park strategically so you could check out every cowboy who strolls in and out of the barn?"

"Oh, I guess it is a good view."

Savannah shook her head and took a big, refreshing drink of her lemonade. "So, when are you going to decide which of these guys you want to stick with?"

"And miss out on the fun of keeping them all guessing? You know, I could ask you the same thing, Miss Queen of the Peach Farm. You could have anyone you wanted, or maybe you've got your eye on a peach-picking farmer."

Savannah gave a short laugh at the idea of falling for anyone who worked on the produce farm, even the entire ranch. They were too old, too young, or married. Well, Luke was good-looking, but she couldn't imagine thinking of him as anything more than a friend.

"I have my hands full without throwing a guy in the mix."

"Yeah, right. I saw you eyeballing Cannon Russell earlier."

"Doesn't hurt to look a little." And Cannon, one of the bull riders, certainly wasn't hard to look at. A long, lean, bull-riding machine. Of course, she wasn't the only one looking. He always had a gaggle of buckle bunnies following him around like a swarm of mosquitoes looking for a taste.

Still, Savannah couldn't stop looking at all the guys. She blamed her sister Lizzie. After all, how could she be around Lizzie and her fiancé, Chris, see how crazy in love they were and not be affected?

"I'd give him a seven."

Savannah pulled herself back from her thoughts and shifted her gaze to Abby. "Seven? Are you blind? He's at least an eight and a half, probably a nine."

"I like to leave a bit of a window on the top end of the scale in case someone ever really knocks my socks off."

They fell into assigning hotness numbers to every cowboy who walked by. When Abby started calling out the numbers loud enough that the cowboys in question could hear them, Savannah wanted to crawl under her hat. When Cannon strolled by and Abby hollered, "Seven and a half," Savannah shushed her and swatted her on the arm. Abby just hooted.

Savannah shook her head and called out, "Don't mind her. Tourette's."

Cannon laughed a little then headed off to talk with some of the other bull riders.

"I don't know why I hang out with you," Savannah said.

"Because you love me."

"So you think."

Abby laughed again and climbed into her living quarters to get ready for the evening's ride. Savannah downed the rest of her lemonade before grabbing her bag to change clothes, too.

When they both emerged from the trailer, the grandstands were filling up and the smell of grilling hamburgers permeated the air. Savannah's stomach growled, but she rarely ate anything close to when she was supposed to ride. Her dinner usually came in the slice of time between when she finished riding and the bull riding event started.

They headed toward the back curve of the arena next to the grandstands, chatting with other competitors along the way.

"Mmm-mmm, your boyfriend is looking good tonight." Abby nodded toward where Cannon was standing with Liam Parrish, a former bronc rider who now ran the company that provided the rough stock and staff for the rodeo.

"You know, the way you keep finding him, I think you might be the one who has the hots for him."

"Not gonna lie. I wouldn't mind sampling his wares, but I'm not fighting the gauntlet of bunnies to do so."

"Savannah?"

She turned at her name to see a good-looking man standing a few feet away. Tall, nicely built and wearing the ubiquitous cowboy hat, jeans and boots. But he wasn't part of the rodeo. She'd been around rodeo competitors for enough years to be able to peg one. Something about him seemed familiar, though, but she couldn't quite place it.

He tipped his tan Stetson back a bit, revealing more of his close-cropped auburn hair and light eyes. "Travis Shepard."

"Oh, hey." She smiled and moved in for a quick hug, noticing that Travis had changed a good bit since she'd last seen him. Taller, built more like a man than a teenage boy, and, wow, he'd certainly grown into a looker. Suddenly feeling uncharacteristically awkward at that thought, she stepped back from him. "How long has it been?"

"A while."

Several years, in fact. She hadn't seen him since right after he'd gotten married and was about to ship out with the army overseas. A lot had changed since then. He'd lost his wife and had traded the military for a private investigator's license. A flicker of something in his eyes made her wonder if he'd just had a similar thought.

"What are you doing here?" she asked.

He nodded toward the arena. "Came to watch my niece Hailey. She's riding in the mutton busting."

"Really? Last time I saw her and Rita, Hailey was still a baby."

"She's six now, and Rita's pregnant again."

Abby cleared her throat, drawing Savannah's attention. When she saw the look of appreciation on Abby's face, Savannah fought the unexpected urge to step in between her two friends, to protect Travis even though from the looks of him he was perfectly capable of taking care of himself. After all, he'd been a soldier.

"Travis and I went to high school together," Savannah said.

She shifted her gaze to Travis, who had taken a couple of steps closer, allowing her to see his eyes better, remember the pretty pale blue. Even when he'd been an awkward teen, he'd had those striking eyes.

"Travis, this is my friend Abby. She's another barrel racer."

Travis smiled and nodded. "I think I've seen you ride before."

"You go to a lot of rodeos?" Abby asked, interest in her voice.

"A few, the nearby ones when Hailey is riding." He shifted his gaze to Savannah. "I won't be surprised if she follows in your footsteps. That girl came out of the womb loving animals and not afraid of anything."

"Sounds more like my sister Carly than me."

Travis grinned. "I don't know. I seem to remember

you having no fear getting on a horse that was twice as tall as you were."

He remembered her that far back? Guilt squirmed inside her that she couldn't remember him earlier than their sophomore year. Of course, she'd been all about rodeo then and probably wouldn't have noticed him if he'd strolled by her wearing blinking lights.

The announcer welcomed everyone to the night's events and got the ball rolling with the opening ceremonies. As Abby and Savannah turned toward the arena for the national anthem, Travis took up a spot next to Savannah. While she should be concentrating on the words to the song and the gently waving American flag being held by the rodeo queen in the middle of the arena, she caught herself glancing out of the corner of her eye at Travis. They'd known each other for years. Why was he suddenly making her all jittery? That was just weird.

She couldn't be attracted to Travis.

Well, why not? She'd been attracted to plenty of guys and never let them know. And though she'd only been talking to him for a handful of minutes, one glance had been enough to show her that the grown-up Travis Shepard was going to turn a lot more female heads than the teenage Travis Shepard ever had.

When the flag bearers left the arena, Savannah shifted her weight. "We should go get ready for our rides."

Instead of moving toward where they'd left the horses, however, Abby propped her foot up on the lowest rail of the fence surrounding the arena and shot Savannah a knowing grin. "We've got plenty of time. We're next to last."

Left with no choice but to join her friend or be obvious about the fact she was trying to get away from suddenly-too-attractive Travis, she leaned her arms along the top of the fence and watched as the little kids were led out on the opposite side of the arena.

"Hard to believe we were ever that little, isn't it?" Travis said from beside her.

"Yeah." Wow, way to be a sterling conversationalist, monosyllabic and everything. But how was she supposed to think clearly when she'd swear she could feel his body heat radiating toward her? She was going to kill Lizzie for putting all those gooey, romantic thoughts in her head.

And then it got worse when Travis leaned close and pointed at a little girl wearing a lime-green Western-style shirt and a mini white cowgirl hat.

"That's Hailey."

"Aww, she's adorable." Look at that, an actual coherent sentence. Maybe the shock of seeing the grown-up version of Travis was beginning to wear off.

They all watched as the first little boy started on his sheep ride only to fall into the dirt about a second later. The next boy did a bit better but not much. The story stayed pretty much the same through three more kids, and then it was Hailey's turn.

"Come on, Hailey," Travis called out then whistled.

Savannah couldn't help but smile at Travis's obvious support of his niece. If Corinne had lived, would he have some little tykes of his own by now? She shook off the sad memory of Corinne's death and refocused on Hailey. The pint-sized girl dug her fingers into the sheep's wool and hugged her body close to its back. As soon as the man holding the sheep let go, the animal took off in an attempt to rid itself of Hailey. But unlike the kids before her, Hailey stuck like glue the full eight seconds and even a few more before she let go. When she hit the dirt, she rolled back up onto her feet and waved at the cheering crowd.

Abby leaned forward and spoke past Savannah to Travis. "That girl's got spunk."

Travis smiled wide, every inch the proud uncle. If he'd been good-looking before, that smile made him devastatingly handsome. Either a miracle of genetics had happened in the past few years, or Savannah had just been blind to anything but her twin goals of good grades and top rodeo times back when she and Travis had crossed paths every day. He hadn't been ugly, but she'd had no inkling that he would one day steal her breath.

They all clapped when Hailey got her blue ribbon.

"Well, I owe a little cowgirl a congratulations kiss," Travis said as Savannah stepped back from the fence.

Damn if her gaze didn't go right to his lips, and her mind to wondering what they would feel like against her own.

Travis met her gaze just as she jerked hers away from his lips.

"Good luck with your run," he said.

"Thanks."

"What, I don't get a 'good luck'?" Abby teased.

Travis broke eye contact with Savannah. "Good luck to you, too, but I gotta admit I'll be pulling for my hometown girl."

A flutter of giddiness zipped through Savannah at the knowledge that not only would Travis be watching her ride, but he'd also be cheering for her. It took a remarkable amount of effort for her to not smile like an idiot, especially when Travis shifted his gaze back to her. Yeah, she needed a good, swift kick or maybe a jolt from a cattle prod.

"It was good to see you again," he said.

"You, too. Tell Rita I said hello, and tell Hailey she's a mighty good rider."

He nodded but then seemed to hesitate for an extra long moment, almost as if he didn't want to leave, before nodding and walking away.

"Whooee, that is one fine specimen right there," Abby said.

Savannah took a moment to bite down on an uncharacteristic comeback that would have sent up red flags for Abby. Heck, the entire grandstand full of people would see those bright flags waving.

Thing was, as she watched Travis walk away, she realized Abby wasn't wrong. He was indeed a fine, fine hunk of man.

"Is he seeing anyone?"

Savannah shrugged, not trusting herself to not tell her friend to back off. She had no right to claim Travis Shepard, not when she'd told Abby she was too dang busy to date. At least not until she'd built the store into the destination she wanted it to be. She'd proven in the past that success required single-minded focus.

What about Lizzie? She was successful, the acting head of the family's large energy company, and still had time for falling in love and starting a family.

Yeah, and she had a lot more employees at her beck and call. And she wasn't building Baron Energies from the ground up.

When Abby started giggling, Savannah finally tore her gaze away from Travis's retreating form. "What?"

"Hope he likes drool," Abby said as she made a circular motion with her finger toward Savannah's mouth. "Because you've got a bloodhound slobber situation going on."

"I do not."

"Really? Let's ask the crowd." Abby made as if she was going to call out a question to the people sitting in the grandstands.

Savannah spun on her heel, gave her friend a playful slug in the arm, and headed toward Bluebell. And she'd never admit in a million lifetimes how difficult it was to not glance over her shoulder and scan the crowd for Travis. Abby didn't need any more ammunition. And Savannah didn't need to have images in her head of Travis rewarding her for posting a good time with a congratulations kiss of her own.

Chapter Two

Travis fought the urge to look back over his shoulder as he walked away from Savannah. Maybe if he ignored the buzzy tug of attraction he'd felt toward her, it would go away. It wasn't the first time he'd been drawn toward Savannah, but he wasn't that smitten boy anymore. And he didn't want to feel anything other than friendship toward her or any other woman.

Besides, he doubted his attraction would end any differently than it had all those years ago. After all, back in high school her focus had been on rodeo and family to the exclusion of everything else. Considering where they were, he'd venture a guess that hadn't changed.

Not that it mattered. Savannah Baron might not have changed, but he had. When they'd been teenagers, he couldn't have imagined the pain and turmoil he had ahead of him, the anger that still accompanied him every day even though he did his best to hide it.

He shoved those hard memories and thoughts of Savannah away as he drew close to his own family. He walked up behind Hailey and lifted her into his arms.

"Hey there, cowgirl. Got a kiss for your favorite uncle?"

Hailey giggled. "You're my only uncle, silly."

"Guess that means I have to be your favorite, huh?"

Hailey leaned over and gave him a big, smacking smooch on the cheek.

"Who were you talking to?" Rita asked as she tucked Hailey's big blue ribbon into her purse.

"Savannah Baron and a friend of hers."

"I haven't seen Savannah in forever."

"Yeah. She said it was when this squirt was a baby." He tickled Hailey's ribs, making her squirm to get away. With a laugh, he set his niece on her feet. She immediately ran over to talk to one of her friends who'd competed in the mutton busting, too.

"So, how is she?" Rita asked. "Still single?"

Travis knew that tone and shook his head at his sister.

"What does that mean? She's not single?"

"It means you can stop those matchmaking thoughts you're having."

Rita crossed her arms. "Why? You liked her once upon a time."

"That was a long time ago. A lot has happened since then. We're not the same people we were then."

"Sure you are, just older and with more experiences."

"Listen, I know you're just looking out for me, doing the big-sister thing, but I don't need dating advice."

"Because you're not dating." A tinge of sadness enveloped her words and shadowed her eyes when she looked up at him.

"No, I'm not." And he had no intention of changing that. Every time he thought about it, his heart got jerked back to the happy days he'd spent with Corinne and how they'd been ripped away in a split second. Going through that once was heart-wrenching. Not just that he'd lost Corinne but how he'd lost her. And the fact he'd lost what might have been—children, a long and happy life together. He wasn't exactly chomping at the bit to set himself up for that kind of pain again. Taking that chance just wasn't worth it.

But damned if his gaze didn't drift across the arena, searching for Savannah anyway.

"You know Corinne wouldn't want you to spend the rest of your life alone. You were much too young when she passed and you have a lot of years ahead of you."

Of course, she couldn't know that. His life could be snuffed out tomorrow, as quickly and unexpectedly as Corinne's had been. But he wouldn't say that and hurt her, especially when Hailey was nearby and might hear. Despite the harsh reality of the world, he wanted nothing more than to keep that away from Hailey for as long as he could.

Wanting to change the subject, he glanced at Rita. "Would you like something from the concession stand?"

Rita let her breath out slowly but didn't pursue the original topic further. "Grab us a couple of burgers and lemonades."

Thankful for the break from his sister's scrutiny, he made his way through the crowd. But leaving behind what Rita had said proved more difficult. There was no denying he'd been immediately attracted to Savannah, a pull he hadn't felt in a long time. Didn't want to feel. Was it even possible for him to move on? Would it be fair to a woman when a chunk of him still clung to the hope of vengeance against the man who'd killed Corinne? That was an ugliness he just couldn't shed, and he doubted Savannah or any other woman would find it appealing.

As he stood in the concession line, he shifted his gaze toward the end of the arena. He couldn't see Savannah, but maybe that was a good thing. What were the chances she was single anyway? She was nice, beautiful, talented and from a well-to-do family. That seemed like a recipe for having guys lined up around the corner.

"What can I get for you?"

Travis jerked his attention back to the woman working the concession stand window. He needed to forget about Savannah Baron now the same way he had when he'd been a hormonal teenager fumbling every attempt to tell her how he felt.

But as he carried the food and drinks back to the grandstand, he began to realize forgetting the second time might not be any easier than it had been the first. Savannah Baron wasn't the type of woman you forgot easily.

"So, I think you need to hunt down Travis after your ride and ask him out," Abby said as she and Savannah prepped Rosie and Bluebell for their rides.

"That will not be happening."

"Why not? He's hot."

That he was. "Be that as it may, I wouldn't feel right about it."

"Why the heck not? If you're too shy to do it, I can ask for you."

Savannah propped her hand on her hip. "What is this, third grade?"

"Pretty sure those kind of sparks don't fly in third grade."

"There were no sparks."

"Oh, yeah, there were definite sparks. I'm somewhat of an expert on the subject."

Savannah rolled her eyes. "Just because you date a lot doesn't make you an expert on everyone else's love life."

"Maybe not, but I've known you long enough to know that you were interested."

Savannah laughed. "Earlier you were convinced I was head over heels for Cannon."

"There's a difference between appreciation and interest."

Savannah laid her palm against Bluebell's neck and stroked the animal. "It wouldn't feel right. Travis lost his wife a few years ago. She was shot in a convenience store holdup."

The teasing fell away from Abby's face. "That's awful."

"Yeah, and he wasn't even here. He was stationed overseas with the army. I can't imagine how horrible it was for him."

Abby glanced toward the crowd watching the tie-down roping as if she could spot Travis among them. "So maybe he could use another friend?"

Though Abby wasn't being callous, Savannah should have known her friend wouldn't give up so easily.

"I'm sure he has friends." Before Abby could say anything else, Savannah pulled herself up into the saddle and guided Bluebell away. If she had any hope of making a good ride, Savannah needed a few minutes to clear her head of thoughts of Travis, the tragedy he'd lived through and the unwise attraction she'd felt toward him.

By the time the barrel racing began, she'd managed to partially clear her head. But she couldn't help a glance at the grandstand, wondering if Travis was sitting among the crowd.

She forced her focus back to the competitors ahead of her. For the next several minutes, she needed nothing else to matter beyond working with Bluebell to make a good, safe ride.

Two spots ahead of her, Abby prepared for her run. Savannah held Bluebell steady as Abby sped into the arena, guiding Rosie expertly around the barrels, shaving precious microseconds off her time. Cheers rang out from the grandstands for Abby, a crowd favorite. As she rounded the last barrel, Abby urged Rosie toward the finish. It struck Savannah that Abby's and Rosie's expressions of determination weren't all that different. They worked as one seamless unit all the way through and beyond the finish line.

Savannah scratched Bluebell between the ears and leaned forward. "Almost time, girl. Let's show Abby and Rosie we can still give them a run for their money."

As Tanya Gonzales made her ride, Savannah took several slow, calming breaths. When Tanya cut the last corner too close and knocked over the barrel, Savannah did her best to push that negative image out of her mind.

When Tanya finished her run and the overturned barrel was righted, Savannah took one last, fortifying breath then kicked Bluebell into a gallop. The horse responded immediately, knowing exactly what to do.

They flew around the first two barrels as if Bluebell had wings and her feet weren't even touching the ground. Sensing a good time, one to rival Abby's, Savannah urged Bluebell to fly even faster. The dirt of the arena, the white fencing, the crowd beyond—it was all a blur as they raced the clock.

Excitement surged through Savannah's veins. This had always been when she felt most free, most in control of her life, as if she was astride Pegasus and letting the world fall away below her.

They rounded the final barrel, and the image of Tanya knocking over the barrel shot to the front of Savannah's thoughts. Before she could prevent it, she stiffened, throwing off the delicate balance between Bluebell and herself.

Savannah gasped as she felt one of Bluebell's feet slip on the loose dirt. In the next moment, she tipped sideways.

It all happened so fast, she was helpless to catch herself. One moment she was having a fantastic ride. In the next, she toppled sideways, hitting the barrel with her ribs. She tried in vain to extricate herself, but she ended up on the ground, her leg pinned beneath Bluebell's heaving body.

Pain shot through Savannah's left side, causing tears to well in her eyes. Before she could catch her breath, she was surrounded by cowboys and Jonesy, the bullfighter.

"Hang on," Jonesy said.

She still fought to take a deep breath as the guys pulled her free of Bluebell. Thankfully, the horse got to her feet.

"Is she okay?" It hurt to speak, but she had to know if Bluebell was injured.

"She looks fine," said Logan Bradshaw, one of the newer pickup guys. "But we'll get her checked."

She blinked a few times against fuzzy vision, and then a paramedic was there checking her for broken bones and signs of concussion.

"I didn't hit my head," she managed to say. "But my side hurts like the devil."

The cowboys made a circle around her as the paramedic pulled up the side of her shirt and examined her ribs. "I don't see any obvious breaks, but you need to get an X-ray. And you'll have some nasty bruising."

Please just let it be a bruise. She hated the idea of having broken ribs, especially with her dad already at the ranch nursing his own rodeo injuries.

After the paramedic was satisfied it was safe to move her, Jonesy and one of the tie-down ropers helped her to her feet.

Jonesy plunked her hat back on her head. "I can think of better ways to get a bunch of guys' attention."

She laughed a little and immediately regretted it as pain

shot from her side through her middle to her back like a hot poker. "Ah, damn you, Jonesy."

"Sorry."

Though she felt as if she'd been dropped off the top of a building, she managed to exit the arena under her own power, if a bit slowly. When the crowd started cheering, she gingerly raised her right hand in acknowledgment. Again, even in the midst of her pain, she wondered if Travis was among them or if he'd gone home after meeting up with Hailey and Rita.

Part of her hoped he'd left. This wasn't exactly her finest moment.

As she exited the arena, Abby was there to meet her. "Damn, girl, you scared me half to death."

"Can't say I want to repeat it myself."

The paramedic tried to guide her toward the ambulance.

"I don't need to ride in the ambulance. Someone else might need it more. I'll just drive to the hospital."

"You really shouldn't be driving, not until you're fully checked out."

"I'll take her," Abby said as they reached the back end of the livestock pens.

"No, I need you to take care of Bluebell, make sure she's okay."

"You heard what the man said," Abby protested. "You took a nasty fall, and you don't need to drive until we see if your brain got knocked loose."

"I can take her."

They looked toward the sound of the male voice. Yep, Travis Shepard stood just beyond the pens. Well, she guessed that answered her question of whether he'd left.

Savannah's heart rate kicked up a couple of notches.

"That's not necessary."

"But it's going to happen anyway." Instead of the boy she'd known, he sounded every inch the army man he'd once been, brooking no argument.

Honestly, she didn't want to argue. She wanted to get the trip to the hospital over with so she could take a hot shower and lie down.

She nodded. "Thank you." Then she shifted her gaze toward where the vet was examining Bluebell.

"Don't worry," Abby said. "We'll take good care of her. You just take care of yourself. And if you need me, call."

Abby nodded then allowed Travis to take her arm to steady her as he guided her out into the field of parked vehicles.

"Sorry to bother you like this," she said.

"It's no bother. What are old friends for?"

"But you don't get to see the rest of the rodeo."

"Savannah, I've been to more rodeos than I can count. And I saw everything I was interested in at this one anyway."

She told herself that he was simply referring to Hailey's ride on the sheep, but a part of her that she fully blamed Abby for wondered if he might be including her in his statement, as well. If so, he was probably mighty disappointed at the moment.

When they reached his SUV, he opened the passenger door and helped her climb in. She winced against the pain, unable to hide it. Once she was seated, she let her head drop back and took a deep breath. But when she felt Travis's hands move close, she jerked upright, causing fresh pain to slice through her.

Travis placed his palm against her shoulder. "Hey, careful. I'm just getting the seat belt."

She felt like a fool for her overreaction, but he simply went about pulling the seat belt across her torso and fastening it, acting as if he hadn't noticed anything out of the ordinary. She wanted to thank him for that but didn't want to draw any more attention to the fact that he made her jumpy.

Honestly, she didn't know why he made her so on edge. They'd known each other for years, even if they hadn't spoken for the past several.

She imagined a miniature version of herself sitting on her shoulder shaking her head. "Of course you know why," her tiny clone said. "He's as hot as a barbecue on the Fourth of July, and you haven't had a real date in way too long."

Savannah closed her eyes, trying to shove the words away. She hoped Travis chalked it up to her being in pain, and not anything to do with his nearness. She suddenly wished she could snap her fingers and transport herself back to the safety and solitude of her apartment above the Peach Pit. There she didn't have to deal with physical pain and a jittery, most unexpected attraction that had thrown her for a loop.

In the distance, she heard the rodeo announcer call the name of the first bull riding contestant followed by enthusiastic cheers from the crowd. Bull riding always came last because it was the most popular of the rodeo events. Normally, she'd be sitting in the stands, too, chomping down on a cheeseburger. Now all she could think about was not breathing too deeply and the fact that she was being hauled to the hospital by a guy who made her heart beat way faster than average. This was *not* how she'd envisioned her night going.

She grunted as he eased his vehicle out of the field.

"Sorry. I'm being as careful as I can," he said.

"I know." Still, she was grateful when he pulled out onto smoother pavement.

"If it makes you feel any better, you were looking good to beat Abby's time before the slip."

She opened one eye as she rolled her head toward him. "Not really."

He smiled, and her heart gave an extra thump as if she didn't already know that Travis Shepard was a very good-looking man.

"What happened?"

"Just lost my concentration for a split second. That's all it takes." She just hoped that the momentary lapse hadn't cost her Bluebell. Sure, the horse had walked out of the arena, but Savannah wouldn't rest easy until the veterinarian gave her mare a clean bill of health. To be such powerful animals, horses were also fragile, more so than even their human riders.

It didn't take long to reach the hospital, but Savannah felt every bump on the way. The pain ricocheted through her body each time the truck hit one.

She didn't move, not even when Travis came around to her side of the vehicle and opened the door.

"Can't I just sit here for the rest of the night?"

"I'd guess they're not going to wheel the X-ray machine out to the parking lot."

"Well, that's mighty inconsiderate of them."

Travis chuckled then reached across her to unbuckle her seat belt. Thankfully, this time she didn't jump at his close proximity. Maybe her brain was finally remembering she wasn't normally so jumpy around men. She was a grown woman who was around guys all the time—farm workers, her brothers, rodeo cowboys.

But none of them came to her rescue like a knight in shining armor, did they?

Oh, for Pete's sake, he'd driven her to the hospital. Any decent human being would have done the same thing.

She seriously needed that hot shower, some ibuprofen and about twelve hours of uninterrupted sleep.

She did her best not to grunt or wince as Travis helped her out of the truck, but her efforts proved futile.

Savannah leaned on his arm more than she wanted to as he helped her toward the E.R. entrance, but she wanted to collapse onto the sidewalk even less. "You had to have better things to do on a Friday night."

"Nah. This is way more exciting than my normal Friday night."

She glanced up at him. "That is one sad state of affairs right there."

Travis laughed. "Don't I know it."

Despite her pain, she managed to elbow him a little bit for his teasing.

Once inside, he helped her to the check-in desk where she was finally able to lean against something other than Travis's distracting warmth. Thankfully, the E.R. was next to empty, and they took her straight back. She glanced over her shoulder in time to see Travis grab a magazine from the rack and settle himself on one of the institutional chairs that was probably about as comfortable as sitting on a boulder.

She gritted her teeth through every movement, but she still didn't think anything was broken. She'd had broken bones before. In fact, the bad break of her wrist that she'd suffered several years ago while riding in Cheyenne had led to her always carrying her ID and medical insurance card in her back pocket, even while she was riding. She didn't want a repeat of having to sit in an emergency room waiting for someone to bring her proof of insurance to her before she could get treated.

As she waited for the X-ray results, her stomach started grumbling, reminding her that she hadn't had anything to eat since she'd left home hours ago. But she was also so tired that she thought there was a pretty good chance she would fall face-first into any plate placed in front of her. At the moment, she'd give up her slice of the Baron inheritance for a candy bar.

She'd finally found a position that was remotely comfortable to sit in when the doctor came into the exam room.

"Good news," he said. "No cracked or broken bones. You do, however, have deep bruising that's going to hurt for a while."

"That I figured out."

He smiled. "You're very lucky because there's also no sign of concussion."

"I've taken enough falls over the years to know to protect my head."

"Just get some rest and take it easy until you heal. Take over-the-counter painkillers as needed."

After thanking the doctor, she headed out to the waiting room to find a pretty nurse talking to Travis. When he spotted Savannah, he looked happy to see her.

"My friend is finished," he said as Savannah approached him.

When the nurse turned and saw her, the petite blonde's features showed disappointment before she returned her attention to Travis. "If you're ever in Mineral Wells again, give me a call."

Travis didn't respond other than to show the nurse a small smile.

Savannah resisted the crazy urge to tell the nurse to scoot as if she was a nosy cat. "Looks like you made a friend while I was gone," she teased.

He made a sound deep in his throat that told her he was

way less interested in the conversation with the nurse than the nurse had been.

Savannah smiled. "I've heard of picking up dates in bars, even at church, but never an E.R. waiting room."

Travis glanced past Savannah then tossed what looked like a business card in the trash. Savannah swallowed any more teasing when she wondered if his resistance to the nurse's advances had more to do with the loss of his wife than anything about the nurse.

Travis bent to retrieve a white paper bag from the burger place down the street.

"If that is for me, you are my new best friend."

"A burger and fries is all it takes? What does the milk-shake get me?"

"A homemade peach pie?"

He nodded. "I call that a good deal."

Her stomach growled again, louder than before.

Travis laughed. "Sounds like I was just in time."

She pointed toward the bag. "Oh, give me that and hush."

She took the first big bite of her burger as they walked out the door of the E.R. A slurp of the chocolate milk-shake followed as Travis's phone rang.

He glanced at the screen and made a "hmm" sound that told her he didn't know who it was. "Hello?"

She nabbed a couple of seasoned fries from the bag as Travis listened to someone say something on the other end of the call.

"Okay." He extended the phone to her. "It's for you."

"Me?"

"Yeah. It's your dad."

Chapter Three

Savannah cursed under her breath. Even before she accepted the phone from Travis, she knew someone had reported back to her dad that she'd been hurt. Sometimes it seemed as if Brock Baron had Big Brother–style eyes everywhere. It proved useful in business but was frustrating if you were his daughter.

"Dad? Why are you calling this number?"

"Because you won't answer your phone."

"It's back in Abby's trailer."

"And you're at the hospital, something you failed to mention to your family."

Figured she'd get hurt at the one rodeo where none of her brothers or Carly was competing.

She stopped walking and had to keep herself from tossing the bag holding her dinner in frustration. "I was a little busy getting an X-ray. And before you ask, I'm fine. Just a bruise."

A monster bruise, but her dad didn't have to know that.

"Why are you with Travis Shepard instead of medical professionals?"

She closed her eyes and took a deep breath before she let fly what part of her wanted to say, the part that she always held at bay. "Because I didn't think a bruise warranted an ambulance ride, especially when the bull riding is much more likely to cause serious injuries that would require an ambulance. I'm *fine*."

"I can send someone to get you."

"No. I'm here to spend the weekend with Abby."

"You're not riding hurt."

She bit her lip because he would have never said that to her brothers. "No, I won't be riding tomorrow, but I can cheer on Abby, hang out with my friends."

Her dad didn't immediately respond, and she wondered if for once he was holding back saying what he was thinking. It was very unlike him, but she didn't want to tempt fate by pointing that out.

"As long as you're sure that you're okay," he finally said.

"I am. Sore, but okay. You know it's not the first time I've taken a spill."

"Come see me when you get home."

He might want to assure himself she was truly not badly hurt, but she couldn't help but wonder if he also was using the opportunity to talk to her about the store. What little she'd eaten grew heavy in her stomach.

When the call ended, she handed the phone back to Travis.

"You all right?" he asked.

"Yeah."

"I've got the feeling I should hire your dad to help me track down people."

"Oh, please do. Obviously, it's something he can do while laid up. Keep him busy."

When Travis gave her a questioning look, she explained. "He was injured several weeks ago in a senior rodeo, so he can't go to work. And let's just say that he doesn't do well with boredom."

"Ah. But you're gone a lot, right?"

She shook her head as he opened the car door for her. "I don't ride as much as I used to. I run the farm store on the ranch."

"Well, you obviously haven't suffered much for not riding as often."

"Ha. You seem to have forgotten the part about me crashing and burning tonight."

Travis shrugged. "We all slip at some point."

"So you have a great P.I. boo-boo story?"

Travis helped her into the SUV and automatically reached for the seat belt. "I do."

"Can it beat falling off a horse in front of hundreds of people?"

"Does following a fugitive and having half a dozen Rottweilers trap you in a tree count?"

The image made her giggle. She lifted her hand to her mouth. "Sorry. What did you do?"

"Before or after I had to call 911 to get help?"

This time she snorted.

"That's it. I'm taking back the milkshake." He reached for it.

"Oh, no, you don't." She pulled the cup out of his reach. A stab of pain in her side caused her to gasp.

"Sorry." Travis placed his hand on her jean-clad leg. "I didn't mean to make you hurt yourself."

"It's okay." Savannah tried not to focus on the feel of his warm hand against her thigh. He wasn't squeezing or pressing down, but she still sensed his strength. And felt an odd tingle, as if his flesh were touching hers.

"If it makes you feel better, you can pour the milkshake over my head," he said.

She forced her focus off the weight of his hand and lifted a brow. "And waste a perfectly good milkshake?"

"Saved by a sweet tooth." Travis smiled as he backed away from her and shut the door.

She tried not to think about how she was simultaneously glad he'd removed his hand while also missing the connection. Jeez, maybe the doctor had been wrong and she did conk her head.

The dose of extra-strength pain reliever she'd been given must be taking effect because the ride back to the rodeo grounds wasn't as painful as the trip to the hospital.

Savannah directed Travis toward Abby's rig. Before he even turned off the engine, Abby came bounding out of the trailer and straight for the passenger side of the SUV.

"Are you okay?" she asked as she opened the door.

Savannah told herself to ignore the twinge of loss that she wouldn't get to enjoy Travis's touch one more time. The truth was she needed to get away from him and the unexpected attraction toward him. "Fine. Just sporting the mother of all bruises. What about Bluebell?"

"She's fine. A scratch, nothing more."

Savannah breathed a sigh of relief. Bluebell wasn't just a horse to her. She was a good friend, family, a trusted partner.

As Savannah unlatched her own seat belt this time and slid out of the truck, Abby spotted her bag of food and milkshake.

"Did you two go to the hospital or out on a date?"

Savannah shot her friend a "What the hell?" look but quickly hid it when Travis appeared at Abby's side.

"Her stomach was growling so much that I was afraid the hospital staff would think a wild animal had gotten loose in the E.R.," Travis said, a mischievous grin on his face.

Savannah wrinkled her nose at him. "Very funny."

Travis gave a little bow, as if on stage. "Thank you. I'll be here all week."

This time, Savannah rolled her eyes and headed toward the trailer. "Well, this chick is done for the day. I'm going to bed and calling do-over for tomorrow."

After shooting Savannah a wicked wink, Abby headed toward the trailer to get the door. When Savannah reached the bottom of the steps, she stopped and half turned toward Travis.

"Thanks for everything."

"You're welcome. Hope you feel better soon. Maybe we can catch up sometime when you're not being carted off to the hospital."

"Yeah." Wow, that sounded enthusiastic. But it was as if her brain had finally said, "Enough. I'm shutting down now." And she had a feeling it had more to do with the hunky version of Travis Shepard watching her than working late the night before or any physical trauma she'd endured.

She finally broke eye contact and climbed gingerly up into Abby's trailer, not quite able to ignore Abby's knowing smile.

"Too bad you're injured," Abby said as she shut the door to the sound of Travis's vehicle starting. "Because you could have jumped that boy and I don't think he would have minded."

Damn if Savannah's face didn't flush at the image that popped into her mind. And of course Abby noticed.

"You do like him."

"He's a nice guy, and yes, he's good-looking. But we're just high school acquaintances who happened to bump into each other."

"Him taking you to the hospital and buying you dinner isn't just bumping into each other."

"He was just being helpful. And it was the Burger Barn, not a five-star restaurant."

"Uh-huh."

"I don't think he's interested in dating anyway, and I don't blame him." She recounted the incident with the nurse.

"Maybe he just wasn't interested in *her*."

With a shake of her head, Savannah left her friend behind and headed for that much-needed hot shower. If she avoided the topic of Travis for a couple of days, Abby would probably forget all about him.

When Savannah finally stepped under the water, it felt as if a week had passed since she'd left home instead of only half a day. She closed her eyes and let her mind float, and her thoughts drifted to Travis. In the solitude of the shower, she allowed herself to think about him, his striking good looks, the strength she sensed in him, the warmth of his hands as he'd helped her in and out of the SUV.

She ran her hand over the spot on her leg where he'd placed his palm, imagining she could still feel it. As her thoughts meandered down one path and then another, she found herself imagining him in the shower with her, water sluicing over both of their naked bodies as they pressed against each other.

Had her sister Lizzie finding love really sparked some sort of similar desire in Savannah?

She ran the soap over her aching body, picturing Travis's hands doing it instead. Her skin grew warm and sensitive as she slid her hand up her torso and across her right breast. The image of Travis's mouth settling against that breast had just formed in her mind when she froze and her eyes popped open.

Her heart skipped a beat as she moved her fingertips

back over the area they'd just skimmed and then probed deeper. She bit her lip as the examination found what she'd feared. A lump, and it wasn't on the side of her injuries.

HIDING HER CONCERN from Abby proved so difficult that Savannah used her injuries as an excuse the next morning to say she was going to head home. "We'll plan another weekend soon. Hopefully, I won't be so accident-prone next time."

"I'll forgive you for abandoning me if you ask Travis out and then tell me all about it."

Savannah gave her friend a friendly punch in the shoulder. "Let it go."

Abby looked over her shoulder as she cooked breakfast. "Don't sit there and tell me you haven't thought about it."

Savannah remembered her imaginings in the shower the night before, before that lump in her breast had torpedoed her ability to think of anything else.

She didn't give Abby the satisfaction of a response. Instead, she nabbed a slice of crisp bacon and headed for the door. But as she drove out of Mineral Wells and pointed her truck toward home, she didn't find any peace in her solitude and wondered if she should have stayed through the second night of competition.

Her thoughts kept drifting to Travis and how nice and easy it had been between them the night before. But then her mind got jerked back to the lump. She imagined it getting larger by the second, making her so anxious she finally pulled over and scrolled through online listings for doctors on her phone. She had a regular doctor as well as a gynecologist, but the irrational fear that her family would find out if she visited either one of them had her searching for another option.

She sat at the rest area making calls until she found not

only an office open to take her call but one that could fit her in on Monday. Glad to have a plan of action, it still felt as if Monday were aeons away.

When she pulled up to the barn on the ranch a couple of hours later, her dad was sitting at the entrance in his wheelchair. As if she needed one more thing to worry about. What was he doing, tracking the GPS on her phone?

She forced herself not to wince or make any sounds signaling pain as she slipped out of the truck and approached him. "Hey, Dad. What are you doing out here?"

"Needed to get out of the house. I'm about to go stir crazy."

That she could understand. If she had shattered bones that prevented her from working, from riding, from even getting around by herself, she'd go bonkers, too.

Savannah looked beyond her father to the interior of the barn and caught the look on her brother Jet's face. Yeah, just as she thought. Her dad had directed that he be brought to the barn to make sure everything was exactly as he wanted it. She still wasn't convinced he hadn't known she would be appearing earlier than she'd mentioned and had set up camp to wait for her.

Choosing not to invite the conversation, she moved to the back of the trailer to let Bluebell out.

"Your brother can take care of that."

She wanted to take her father up on the offer, but she refused to do anything that would show she was hurt worse than she'd indicated on the phone the night before. Or to give any clue that anything else was wrong.

"I'm good." As if to negate her words, a sharp pain skewered her side as she opened the trailer. Thankfully, her back was to her father because this time she couldn't prevent gritting her teeth.

Forcing her expression to relax, she guided Bluebell

out of the trailer just as Julieta, her stepmother, pulled up in her SUV.

"You don't look any worse for wear," Julieta said as she got out of the vehicle, looking just as lovely in jeans and a casual pink blouse as she did when wearing her sharp business suits at the Baron Energies office. "To listen to your father last night, I expected you to be rolled home in a full body cast."

Brock huffed. "You are exaggerating."

Julieta lifted a dark brow at him. "I know what I heard."

Savannah hid a smile. Julieta might be considerably younger than Brock, but she wasn't only a pretty face. She could hold her own with her husband despite his tendency to be gruff and demanding. Brock acted put out with Julieta's sass sometimes, but Savannah knew the truth was he admired it even if he never said so.

"I'm glad you're okay," Julieta said to Savannah before turning toward her husband. "Now, you, in the car. Time for your follow-up appointment."

"I'm fine."

"Then this should go quickly." Julieta wasn't letting him talk his way out of going to the doctor as instructed.

Her father was still grumbling as Savannah led Bluebell into the barn. At least his imminent departure would give Savannah a reprieve, however brief, from the conversation about the store.

She ached, was bone tired from not sleeping well the night before, and her stomach was in knots and likely would be until she saw the doctor on Monday.

Jet reached for Bluebell's reins. "I'll take care of her."

"I can do it."

"You can also go home and get some rest. I know you're hurting and were hiding it just now."

Savannah let the facade drop away. "I do sort of feel as if I've been body slammed by King Kong."

He nodded his head toward the barn's entrance. "Go rest while you can."

"Thanks."

But no matter how hard she tried, she couldn't find anything beyond the most superficial sleep for the rest of the weekend. By Monday morning, she felt dreadful, wrung out like a wet cloth. She was ready to cut the lump out of her breast herself just so she could get away from it.

By the time she was being led back to be examined by a doctor she'd never met, she felt as if she was going to hurl. It suddenly occurred to her that she needed to explain her injuries before a nurse or the doctor thought she had been beaten.

The nurse, a peppy young woman named Becky, led her to an examination room. "There's a gown on the table. The doctor will be with you shortly."

"By the way, I have some significant bruising, so tell the doctor not to be shocked. I was in a rodeo Friday night and took a nasty spill."

A hint of suspicion flickered in the nurse's eyes, and Savannah couldn't blame her. She knew lots of women came in with injuries from domestic violence that they tried to pass off as something else.

"You can check with the hospital in Mineral Wells, and with anyone who was at the rodeo."

Becky finally nodded and headed out of the room.

One of the worst things in the world was sitting in a hospital gown in a chilly room waiting forever for a doctor to make an appearance. If she hadn't been so incredibly anxious, she would have brought a book to read.

She wouldn't have thought it possible, but her anxiety level increased after the doctor came in and started her examination. When she finished, Dr. Fisher sat on a rolling stool in front of a laptop and started asking a battery of questions.

"Do you do regular breast self-exams?"

"Have you ever had a mammogram?"

"Is this the first time you've found a lump?"

Savannah answered all the questions, wishing the doctor would instead just tell her it was nothing to worry about.

"Do you have a family history of breast cancer?"

Savannah opened her mouth to answer as she had with all the other questions, but nothing came out.

"Miss Baron?"

"I don't know. Not that I'm aware of."

"If possible, check with your parents."

That was going to be difficult since she had no desire to talk to her father about the lump, not when he'd overreacted about her falling off a horse. Oh, and the fact that she had no idea where her mother was, or if she was even alive, would make it difficult to ask her.

She fell so deep into her thoughts of her mother that she nearly missed what the doctor said next—that Savannah was being sent for a mammogram. Not next week, not the next day, but in a few minutes. That wasn't good, was it? They always made you wait for these things, making you live in a perpetual state of freaking out until the test was done and results received.

As she maneuvered the hallways of the clinic to the mammography area, she felt as if she were trudging through a dense fog that slowed her thoughts while making it seem as if they were racing at the same time. A part of her buried deep inside wished she had her mother beside her, holding her hand. But that wasn't possible. Delia

Baron had abandoned her and her siblings, walked away from them and their dad as if they meant nothing.

Savannah pushed thoughts of her mother away. She'd stopped trying to figure out the why behind her mother leaving a long time ago. After all, she couldn't think of a single reason that wasn't at its core purely selfish. Add in the fact that her father refused to even speak Delia's name, and gradually she just stopped coming up in conversation anymore. Honestly, until Lizzie had gotten pregnant and started worrying about not being a good mother, it had been a while since Savannah had even spared her mom a thought.

But now, as she endured the boob smashing that every woman dreaded, she couldn't help but think about the mystery of her family medical history on her mother's side. As she left the clinic half an hour later with assurances that she'd be contacted as soon as the test results were available, she couldn't stop wondering about her mother. Where was she? Was there a history of breast cancer in her family? Had her mother ever found a lump?

A part of Savannah desperately hoped the answer to that last question was yes, and that it had proven to be nothing of concern. In that one way, she was totally fine with following in her mother's footsteps.

But how was she supposed to find out those answers without cluing her family in to the fact that something was going on?

She was still searching for that answer as she maneuvered through traffic toward the downtown Dallas office of Baron Energies. Even as she walked through the glass entrance and flashed her security badge to the guard at the front desk, she wasn't sure how she was going to casually bring up their mother in conversation with her sister.

As she neared Lizzie's office, she spotted her father's

longtime secretary, Maria, chatting with Emory, who worked as Lizzie's assistant.

Maria's face lit up the moment she saw her. "Savannah, dear, I haven't seen you in forever."

Savannah was careful not to allow Maria to hug her too tightly. "It's good to see you, too." She glanced toward Emory. "Both of you. Is my sister available?"

Lizzie poked her head out of her office door. "So I'm not hearing things. What are you doing here?"

"What, I'm not allowed to come take my sister to lunch?"

It was no wonder Lizzie was surprised by Savannah's appearance considering Savannah rarely darkened the door of the oil company's headquarters. Like Jet and Carly, she had little interest in the energy side of the family business.

Savannah crossed her arms. "Convince me you're not hungry, and I'll leave."

Lizzie shook her head. "You know I can't do that."

"I know. Chris says all you do is eat."

Shock registered on Lizzie's face. "He does not."

"Are you sure about that?"

"If he said that, he's going to wish he never had."

Savannah couldn't help but laugh, which was a minor miracle considering what had propelled her here in the first place. "Okay, so maybe I made that up. I don't think Chris would ever be stupid enough to think that, let alone say it. But I've seen you eat recently. You can put away an impressive amount of food."

"Just for that, you're paying for lunch."

"Really? You're the company bigwig now."

"And you're the one teasing the pregnant lady." Lizzie disappeared into her office but was back a moment later with her purse. Now that her pregnancy was out in the open, she'd gone shopping for maternity clothes. But she made even those look stylish. "Come on. I feel as if I could eat an entire cow."

They didn't go far, just down the block to one of Lizzie's favorite restaurants. When they'd placed their orders, Lizzie leaned back and pinned Savannah with a questioning look.

"So why are you really here?"

"What's with the interrogation?"

"Because you are somewhere other than on a horse or behind the counter of the store."

"I just wanted to get away for a bit, spend some time with my sister before motherhood and marriage gobble you up."

"Dad's still being a pain, huh?"

Savannah shrugged. "I can manage Dad. Avoidance works well, I've found. Though if he were to heal overnight and suddenly go back to work, I wouldn't object."

Lizzie held up her hands in surrender. "Okay, no more looking for ulterior motives."

"Thank you."

Lizzie grabbed a slice of toasted sourdough bread from the basket and dipped it in olive oil. "Heard you took quite a tumble the other night. Frank Owens in Accounting was at the rodeo and said he was surprised you were able to walk out of there on your own."

"So that's who called Dad?"

Lizzie shrugged. "He didn't say, but I wouldn't be surprised. He always has had his lips firmly attached to Dad's behind."

Savannah snorted just as she was taking a drink of water. Embarrassment flooded her cheeks as she tried to cover up her gaffe with her cloth napkin. "Warn a girl next time, would ya?"

Lizzie gave her an evil grin.

They talked some about Lizzie and Chris's plans for the baby's nursery, and it was obvious from how Lizzie's face lit up every time she said Chris's name that she was in love with him. It was great to see, but Savannah found it hard to imagine opening up that much to someone. When you loved another person, they held the power to hurt you. She had to look no further than her father for that.

One wife had walked out on him, and another had died. Though Savannah cared a lot for Julieta, she had to wonder if her dad was crazy for marrying a third time. Was being in love really worth all that pain? She liked things over which she had control. Still, she couldn't deny the happiness her sister had found with Chris.

"I'm happy for you," Savannah said. And maybe even a little envious, despite her best intentions. Her thoughts drifted to Travis, and she wondered what he was doing right in that moment, if he'd thought of her any since they'd parted company. But why would he?

"Thanks," Lizzie said. "I guess you're next up."

"Lord, you sound like Abby."

"And let me guess—she has some long, lanky cowboy picked out for you."

"No, actually. I happened to bump into Travis Shepard at the rodeo, and she suddenly thinks we're destined to be together."

"Why does she think that?"

Savannah shrugged. "I don't know. All I did was talk to him for a few minutes." She didn't mention the fact that he'd taken her to the hospital, waited for her, gotten her dinner and escorted her back to Abby's trailer. But who was keeping track? Like he'd said, that's what old friends were for.

"Well, there could be worse pairings. I saw Travis several months ago while he was eating dinner with Rita and her husband. Travis wouldn't be difficult to look at every day."

"We barely know each other anymore. And what is it with you? You've never been Mary Matchmaker before."

"What can I say? Being in love is a wonderful feeling. Is it a bad thing to wish it for my sister, as well?"

Thankfully, their meals arrived then, and Savannah was able to steer her sister to different topics. But despite being hungry, Savannah couldn't force down more than half her grilled salmon and mushroom risotto, and she loved risotto. She waited until Lizzie, who was eating for two, had finished before she ventured into the real reason for the lunch while trying to hide that fact from her sister.

"Since you got pregnant, has it made you think about Mom?"

Lizzie paused in wiping her mouth. "What brought that up?"

"Nothing. I just had a dream about her the other night."

Lizzie placed her napkin slowly atop her empty plate. "Yeah, I started thinking about her when I found out. I still worry some about being like her, but knowing Chris will be right there beside me helps." Lizzie paused and picked at the edge of the napkin. "I was sad for a bit that my child wouldn't know his or her grandmother, but then I realized that Julieta will fill that role just fine."

"Where do you think she might be now?"

Lizzie shook her head. "No idea. You'd have to ask Dad."

Savannah wanted to do that about as much as she wanted to ride a bull with a hornet's nest tied to its tail. They'd all learned long ago that the topic of their mother was one best left alone.

Lizzie's forehead wrinkled as she stared at Savannah. "What is this really about?"

Savannah grasped for a plausible answer. "Guess I was just thinking about the past after seeing Travis. I found myself wondering how he got beyond losing Corinne." In reality, she didn't think he had.

"It's not the same thing. Corinne had no choice in her leaving her loved ones behind. Mom did."

Savannah could tell by the strained tone of Lizzie's voice that the memories hurt her sister, and she was suddenly sorry for dredging them up. After the scare Lizzie had endured when she'd started spotting early in her pregnancy, she didn't need anything to stress her out. There had to be another way to find the information Savannah needed. She let the subject drop, but it left an awkwardness hanging between her and Lizzie.

"I'm sorry, but I've got to run," Lizzie said as she stood. "I've got a conference call in a few minutes."

Savannah stood and hugged her sister. "Sorry if I ruined lunch."

"You didn't."

Savannah wasn't so sure as she watched her sister walk toward the exit, her shoulders tense.

After paying the bill, Savannah followed in her sister's wake, walking slowly down the sidewalk toward where she'd parked. Even though people passed by her going both directions, business people, tourists, shoppers, she couldn't recall ever feeling so alone. It was an odd feeling for someone who'd often found comfort in solitude, but then it had always been on her terms, in familiar surroundings. A solo ride or getting lost in baking or crafting was a nice reprieve sometimes. Now, the weight of all she hid, of the unknown, hung inside her. She yearned for some lessening of the pressure.

But telling anyone in her family about her fears wouldn't help. In fact, she had no doubt that they would smother her with caring, with questions, with the inability to give her space when she needed it. What they couldn't give her were the answers she needed. No one could except the one family member who was no longer a part of her life.

She slid into her truck and leaned her head back to stare at the ceiling. How did you find a person who obviously didn't want to be found?

Travis's smiling face materialized in her mind, causing her to jerk upright. Could he be the answer to her problem? She'd never been much of a believer in any fate other than what a person made for herself, but what were the odds she'd cross paths with a private investigator, one she knew, right when she needed help finding her mother?

She grabbed her phone and did a search for Travis's P.I. firm. When she found the number, all she could do was stare at it. Did she really want to do this? Couldn't she just wait and find out about her condition once the test results were back? Finding out her family history wasn't going to change the end result one way or another.

But that wasn't all that was going on, was it?

She might have been telling herself for the past two days that the reason she needed to find Delia Baron was medical, but that wasn't the only reason. After years of keeping her feelings about her mom buried so deep she'd forgotten they even existed, that stupid lump in her breast had brought them surging to the surface. She needed to find her mother and ask the one question that really mattered.

Why did you leave us?

Chapter Four

Savannah chickened out. Part of her wasn't sure she wanted to know where her mother was, why she'd up and abandoned her family with no explanation beyond a short note saying she needed to be alone. So instead of calling Travis, she went home and buried herself in the familiar comfort of baking. She'd seen a recipe for peach cake online and already had several ideas of how to adjust it to make it uniquely her own.

Gina had the afternoon off, so Savannah was alone in the store. She had HGTV playing on the TV and was in the midst of pouring cake batter into pans when the front door opened. She was about to call out that she'd be with the customer in a moment when she noticed it was her dad being pushed in his wheelchair by Juan, one of the farmhands.

When Juan shot Savannah an apologetic look, her stomach sank. Her frustration wasn't helped by the file folder sitting on her father's lap. She broke eye contact and took a deep breath as she finished scraping the batter into the pans, then rinsing the bowls in the large sink.

Juan parked her dad at one of the small tables then made himself scarce.

"Can I get you something, Dad?"

"No, I'm good. But we do need to talk about the store."

This so wasn't what she needed today. For a moment, she wished she hadn't made the decision to cut back on her racing. And she hated feeling that way because she loved her dad. At heart he was a good guy, but he had trouble believing anyone else could run a business as well as he could. Lizzie had already been down this road with him before he finally acknowledged that Baron Energies was in good hands while he healed.

She didn't rush to his side, which no doubt annoyed him. Instead, she took the time to put the cakes in the oven, set the timer, and pour both her father and herself sodas before slipping onto a chair opposite him.

"I know the store has been your pet project, but we have to look at financial feasibility, and the store just isn't cutting it."

"We're doing fine." Of course, "fine" wasn't anywhere near good enough for Brock Baron.

"Really? You don't seem to be overrun with customers."

Savannah held back the snappish retort that almost flew past her lips. Instead, she calmly said, "We had an entire bus full of people in here about an hour ago. I completely sold out of peach turnovers and pies."

"That's all well and good, but we're a farm. We should be selling our products directly to food companies."

"We already do that, Dad, and you know it. We're doing quite well in that area."

"Which just proves my point that we should direct all the products that direction."

"I don't think we're quite at the point of throwing up the white flag just yet. The store's offerings are growing every day. In fact, I just put some new cakes in the oven. I'll even bring you one later."

"You're not hearing me. The store is not a wise investment."

Savannah's hold on her frustration slipped. "Well, I think you're wrong."

Shock registered on her father's face. He wasn't used to people disagreeing with him. Before he could say anything, she pressed forward.

"Dad, you trust Lizzie to keep things running well at the office. I'm a grown woman, too. Trust me to know what I'm doing here."

She could tell he didn't like being contradicted, and in that moment she wondered if her mom's leaving hadn't had anything to do with her children at all. Had Brock driven his wife away with his unyielding ways?

"Dad, do you know where Mom is?"

He jerked as if she'd slapped him. "Why would you ask me that?"

"Curiosity. You never say anything about her, and I was so young that I don't remember a lot."

"All you need to remember is that your mother couldn't be bothered to stay and take care of her family."

"But why?"

"Don't know and don't care. Now drop it."   .

Anger welled up inside Savannah, threatening to choke her. The man before her might be her father, but she wasn't a child anymore and didn't appreciate being treated like one. But she held her tongue. Instead, she stood and walked to the door. When she opened it, she spotted Juan leaning against the fender of one of the farm's trucks.

"Juan, my dad is ready to leave now."

She didn't make eye contact with her father as she headed back toward the kitchen. But she didn't stop there. She took the stairs up to her apartment and resisted the urge to slam the door behind her. Rather, she leaned against it and listened until she heard the truck engine outside drive away.

Frustrated with every turn her life had taken the past few days, she slammed the side of her fist back against the door as she let out a growl. With a shake of her head, she crossed the main room of her apartment and stared out the window toward the rows of peach trees in the distance. She loved this ranch, loved her father, the rest of her family, but right now she felt alone and adrift. She wanted answers, and if her father wasn't willing to give them to her, she would turn to someone who could.

She pulled her phone from her pocket and dialed Travis Shepard's number.

TRAVIS FINISHED TYPING the last paragraph of his report, wrapping up a fraud investigation for an art dealer. Though it had been a good-paying gig, he wasn't sorry to have it behind him. Fitting in with the art world muckety-mucks had required his best acting abilities to date.

He heard Blossom, his office manager, answer the phone in the next room. He hit Send on the report and closed the file on his computer as Blossom, the sister of an army buddy, went through her normal speech.

"Hold, please," she said. "Fresh meat, line one."

"I really hope no one but me ever hears you say that," he said.

"Give me some credit."

He laughed a little as he picked up the phone and hit the button for line one. "Travis Shepard."

When he didn't hear any response, he glanced at the phone to see if he'd punched the right button.

"Um, Travis, it's Savannah Baron."

Of all the people who could have been on the other end

of the call, Savannah was near the bottom, right above the president and Kate Upton.

"Hey, good to hear from you. How are you feeling?"

"Like I fell off a horse."

He smiled. "Makes sense."

"It could have been worse. Listen, do you have any time in your schedule to meet up for a drink later today?"

The only thing more surprising than Savannah calling him was her asking him out for a drink. He wasn't sure how he felt about it. Sure, he'd thought of her a lot since seeing her Friday night. He'd even reached for the phone a couple of times, almost calling her to see how she was doing. He kept thinking about their high school years when he'd had a big crush on her and had fumbled every lame attempt to let her know it.

But that was a long time ago. He wasn't that awkward boy anymore, but he also wasn't interested in dating. Of course, he was likely getting ahead of himself. Savannah hadn't given him any sign she was attracted to him anyway. And he'd been the one to suggest they catch up sometime.

"Sure. Want to meet at the Longhorn?" The Longhorn Saloon had been around well before either of them had been old enough to drink.

"No. I'm actually coming into the city, so maybe somewhere near your office."

Something sounded off to his trained ear, as if she didn't want to be seen with him. But considering how her father had tracked her down via Travis's phone, he didn't really blame her. He doubted any of the Baron siblings made a single move that Brock Baron didn't know about. Travis sent up a quick thank-you that his parents had always been the trusting sort.

"Okay. How about Mack's? It's only a couple of miles from here. I can text you the address."

"Sounds good. Is about six too late?"

He laughed a little. "There is no such thing as regular hours in this line of work, so six is fine."

When he hung up, he leaned back in his chair. Once again, his thoughts drifted to a decade before, to when he'd sat in class and sneaked glances at Savannah across the room. She always had an intensity about her, as if she were concentrating hard on something.

His attempts to let her know how he felt lined up like a row of train cars crashing into each other. There was the time he'd managed to get himself paired with her for an English project only to find out that she was going with her family to the National Finals Rodeo in Las Vegas and would have to email him her part of the assignment. Then there was when he'd maneuvered close enough to her at their lockers so he could ask her to prom. But Dillon Brooks had beaten him to it by moments.

Travis had no one to blame but himself for hesitating. At least he had the consolation of hearing Savannah decline Dillon's invitation.

Eventually, Travis quit trying. He still hadn't been the most confident guy in the world when he'd met Corinne the summer after high school, but he'd managed to scrape together enough courage to ask her out. And miracle of miracles, she'd said yes. Within a year they were married and he was headed off to a military career, much to his parents' surprise.

The army had changed him. Somewhere in the midst of boot camp he'd grown a pair and found a well of self-confidence he hadn't known existed until his drill sergeant had screamed it to the surface.

He glanced at the picture of him with Corinne on their

weekend honeymoon in San Antonio. They were riding in one of the boats that carried tourists along the River Walk and grinning ear to ear like the fool kids they were. They had no idea what lay ahead of them. It wasn't fair that he'd voluntarily gone into a war zone, but she'd been the one cut down before her life really got started.

Travis jerked his gaze away from the photo and ran his hand over his face. He'd told himself a long time ago that he should have only happy memories when he thought of Corinne, but sometimes the darkness took over, the hatred that made him want to break into the state penitentiary and rip David Crouch apart. It wasn't enough that Crouch would spend the rest of his life in prison. Travis wanted him to suffer.

He knew it wasn't healthy to carry those types of violent thoughts around inside him, but no matter how hard he tried they never totally went away. The best he could do was push them aside for a little while.

Shifting his focus away from the past, he glanced at the clock. Too early to leave to meet Savannah.

"So, what kind of case got tossed your way this time? Spying on a cheating husband? Someone faking a back injury to get the insurance payout?"

"No case. Just catching up with an old friend." He scrunched his forehead when he caught sight of Blossom, clad head to toe in leather, which he knew she hadn't been wearing a few minutes earlier. It was a striking contrast against her bobbed, dark red hair. "Am I running a P.I. firm or an S&M store?"

She crossed her arms and leaned against the door frame. "Very funny. I told you I was going to see Metallica tonight."

He shook his head. "I can't figure you out. One night

you're going to see One Direction, another Metallica. Do you ever give yourself whiplash?"

"I don't like to be predictable."

"Well, you've got that covered."

She smiled. "You know you like me just the way I am."

"You definitely keep things interesting. What's next, a monster truck rally?"

She wrinkled her nose. "Even I have limits."

He laughed as she turned and headed toward the outer door that led to the elevator lobby.

"I hear Weird Al's coming to town," he called after her.

She spun to walk backward and stuck her tongue out at him.

He chuckled some more as Blossom left. She was right. He wouldn't change one thing about her. He admired how she marched to her own slightly offbeat drum. Every day was an adventure, from what color her hair was going to be to her various exploits. Whether she was learning Irish step dancing or going skydiving, nothing ever surprised him. During his entire tour in Afghanistan, Blossom's brother Kurt had read her letters to the guys and then sworn his sister had to have been left on the doorstep because she was nothing like anyone else in the family.

Travis hadn't been fooled. Kurt loved his sister and looked forward to hearing about her crazy life. She'd originally come to work for Travis so she could save up money to backpack through Europe. But she'd never left, and she'd proven to be an asset time and again. She had a unique insight into why people did the things they did, and she was especially useful when a case called for him to try to figure out the thought processes of women. Even though he'd grown up with a sister and had been married, he'd yet to figure out why women did the things they did.

He made a couple of calls on other cases before finally

closing up shop and heading to Mack's. And damned if he didn't get a little nervous when he walked through the door of the neighborhood restaurant and bar to see Savannah already waiting for him. It was almost enough to make him turn around. Telling himself there was no reason to feel anything other than happy to see an old friend, he approached the booth where she sat.

"You're early," he said.

"Left some time for traffic then didn't run into any."

Again, her words seemed innocent enough, but he sensed a layer of fabrication. Side effect of his job, being able to tell when someone wasn't being totally truthful. What was harder to discern was why. He slid into the booth as he tried to figure it out. Just because she wasn't being completely truthful didn't mean she was trying to hide anything from him—definitely not that she was so anxious to see him that she'd arrived a good ten minutes before their appointed time.

Even though he'd spent a good chunk of an evening with her only a few nights before, it struck him anew how attractive she was. Her dark hair with a slight wave came halfway down her neck, and those pretty blue-gray eyes had probably caught the attention of many a cowboy. It wasn't the first time he'd had those types of thoughts about Savannah, but if anything she'd grown even more beautiful since high school. She wasn't a girl anymore but rather a woman, one who would turn heads anywhere she went.

He told himself that he was simply making observations, nothing more.

Savannah grabbed a menu. "So what's good here?"

"Mack's is famous for the garlic fries."

"Sounds good." Savannah seemed distracted and appeared more fidgety than she ought to be.

"Is something wrong?"

She exhaled and laid the menu flat in front of her. "I want to hire you to find my mother."

He didn't know what he'd expected her to blurt out, but that certainly wasn't it. "Your mother?"

"Yes. She left when I was young, and now I want to know why."

A part of him he didn't want to acknowledge was disappointed that her reason for calling him was professional, but it was for the best. Still, when he saw the layer of desperation in Savannah's eyes, he found himself wanting to erase it. He knew what it felt like to want to find someone that badly, though their reasons were different. "Okay."

"So how does this work?"

"First, I need for you to compile for me anything that could help in the search. Any documents, photos of your mother, anything you remember that could point toward where she might have gone."

"It's been so long. What are the chances she's still even there?"

"We won't know until we check. But even if she's moved on, it's a place to start."

She nodded and pulled a small spiral notebook and pen from her purse. She flipped it open and looked as if she were about to start writing.

Without thinking, he reached across the table and placed his hand atop hers. "You don't have to do it right now."

"The sooner we get started, the sooner you find her."

"We're not going to find her tonight. And I don't know about you, but I'm hungry. Sort of like you were after your trip to the hospital the other night. You're not going to make me starve, are you?"

For a moment, he thought she might argue. But she finally slid her hand from beneath his and moved the notepad to the side, though not back into her purse.

After they ordered the largest basket of garlic fries Mack's sold and a couple of beers, Travis leaned back against the booth. "So, was your dad waiting for you when you returned from Mineral Wells?"

"Yes and no. He was at the barn, but thankfully my stepmother wheeled him off to a doctor's appointment soon after I got back."

"Guess it's hard for parents to realize their kids have grown up sometimes. My mom still tries to slap cartoon character bandages on my boo-boos. It's as if she missed the memo that I've actually served in a war zone."

"I can't say that my dad even knows where the bandages are in his house."

"More of a mom thing."

"I suppose."

He heard the pain in her voice even though she likely had no idea she was telegraphing it. "I'll do my best to find your mom. It'll help if your dad, brothers and sisters share anything they remember, as well."

She was shaking her head even before he finished. "No one can know about this. I don't want them to be aware that I'm looking…in case I don't find anything."

He knew she was hiding something again, but he didn't question her about it. Her reasons for wanting to find her mother weren't relevant to his search, though part of him was intensely curious.

"Okay."

"Is this like lawyer-client privilege? You can't tell anyone what we talk about?"

"You don't want me to say anything, I won't."

She sighed in obvious relief.

He decided to steer totally clear of the topic of the

search, allowing her time to calm down from whatever had her so nervous. Was it her father? Would he frown on the search for the wife who had left him? Travis didn't know all the details of what had happened, but he remembered a comment here and there when he'd been growing up about how Savannah's mom had just disappeared. But it hadn't been suspicious; it had been of her own accord. He couldn't imagine his mother leaving him, Rita and their dad behind. But then he didn't have all the details. He'd have to dig them up soon in order to help Savannah, and he had a feeling she wasn't going to like the process.

For now, however, he was just going to eat fries with her and try to have a nice evening. Remind himself that he shouldn't be thinking about how pretty she was.

"So, tell me more about the store you run. I haven't been out by your family's place in years."

The tension lines on her face relaxed some as she grabbed a fry from the freshly delivered basket. "We sell peaches and pecans from the farm, products made from them, some crafts. It's small now, but I have plans to expand if my dad lets me."

"He still has a say-so over it?"

"Though I'm in charge of the farm's operations, he's still the owner. I didn't hear a peep out of him until he got hurt."

"I learned when I was in the army that the best way to get people on your side is to make them think everything was their idea in the first place."

"Somehow I can't see my dad believing it was his idea to make peach pies."

"Peach pies, huh? Maybe I'll request one of those as part of my payment. In fact, I think I'm still owed one from the other night."

When Savannah glanced up at him, she thankfully

smiled at his comment. "That can be arranged. I might throw in a pecan pie as a bonus."

"Good thing I don't request desserts as all of my payments or I'd look like a linebacker for the Cowboys."

Savannah chuckled then took a drink of her beer. "So you like being a P.I.?"

"I seem to be pretty good at it."

"But do you like it?"

He shrugged. "Most days. Sucks when I confirm a spouse is cheating and I know it's going to lead to a divorce where kids are involved."

He knew he'd said the wrong thing when Savannah didn't respond and dropped a fry back into the basket. Damn it. "Sorry."

She shook her head. "No, it's okay. I have no idea if that's why my parents split or not."

He leaned his forearms against the top of the thick wooden table painted with the labels of various brands of beer. "Why are you looking for your mother now, after all this time?"

Savannah ran her fingertip around the lip of her bottle, and something about that motion made him wonder what it would feel like if she did it against his skin. He jerked his gaze away from her fingers and focused on the fries, shoving three in his mouth.

"Just seemed like the right time."

Again, the conversation veered in other directions. She shared that her friend Abby had won the barrel racing competition at Mineral Wells, that Lizzie was going to have a baby and that she and Carly were in a prolonged friendly argument over which of them was going to be the kid's favorite aunt.

"From what I remember, Carly's the one most likely to get the kid in trouble."

Savannah snorted a laugh. "You're not wrong there."

He liked the sound of Savannah's laugh, even more so when he was the one to make her do so. A distant tolling of a warning bell tried to get his attention, but he ignored it. He told himself that this was nothing more than friends having a nice time, rekindling a friendship.

Yeah, right. He hadn't been thinking of Savannah Baron in a friends-only way since Friday night, no matter how hard he tried. The dream he'd had the night before definitely was more than friendly.

"I should get going," she said after a couple of hours, a single beer, two cups of coffee and the entire huge basket of fries. "You might keep a lot of night hours, but work starts early on a farm."

Before she could pull her wallet from her purse, he pitched enough cash to cover everything on the table.

"I can pay for my share. I should probably cover yours, too."

"You're not exactly an expensive date."

She tensed momentarily, but he didn't backtrack. Evidently concluding he didn't mean anything by it, Savannah smiled and slid out of the booth.

Travis followed her out to the parking lot then pulled a business card from his wallet. He extended it to her. "Just email me with whatever you can think of, and I'll get right on it."

"Thank you," she said. "For everything."

He tapped the edge of his Stetson. "I'm here to serve."

"Working hard for that peach pie, huh?"

He smiled as he realized his heart was lighter than it'd been in a long time. "You have no idea."

As he waved at her as she drove out of the parking lot, he admitted to himself that, wise or not, peach pie was the least of what he wanted from Savannah Baron.

Chapter Five

Savannah yawned as she put a new batch of peach preserves on the store shelves. She felt as if she hadn't slept in a month.

"You look tired," Carly said as she helped herself to a peach muffin.

Her sister had arrived from her home in Houston a few days earlier for an extended stay to help out with their dad as he recuperated. Even though Savannah would have never wished the injury on her dad, she was happy to have Carly around for a while. She didn't see her sister near often enough.

"Didn't sleep well last night," Savannah said. Or the night before, or the night before…

"Your side still hurting?"

At the mere mention of her injury, the humongous bruise ached. "Yeah. I wake up every time I roll over on that side."

Not to mention she'd stayed up late compiling everything she could remember about her mother, scanning old photos and digging out documents. And then she'd lain in bed alternating between worrying about keeping the search from her family and remembering the warm strength she'd felt in Travis's hand when he'd placed it atop hers during their meeting.

"Maybe we should strap you down so you can't move."

Savannah glanced at her younger sister and saw the mischievous smile Carly wore more often than not. She pointed at the large muffin in Carly's hand. "You owe me $2.50 for that, you mooch. You're as bad as Alex. At least he's just a kid."

Julieta's five-year-old son had a sweet tooth the size of Texas, and Savannah indulged it whenever given the chance.

Instead of forking over the money, Carly sauntered to Savannah's side and gave her a smacking kiss on the cheek. "You would charge your favorite sister for her breakfast?"

Savannah rolled her eyes as Carly took a big bite of her muffin and started perusing the stock on the shelves, including some old jars Savannah had spray painted red, white and blue for the upcoming Memorial Day and Fourth of July holidays.

The truth was she did love Carly. They, more than any of their siblings, had gotten lost in the shuffle that began with their mother's leaving and continued through their dad's subsequent marriages. But instead of directing all her energy into school and barrel racing, as Savannah had, Carly had chosen another way to deal with her emotions. She wasn't known as the wild child of the Baron clan for nothing. But even with their vastly different personalities, Savannah felt closer to Carly than anyone else in her family.

The front door opened, drawing Savannah's attention. When recognition kicked in, her heart threatened to stop beating. Standing in the doorway looking as sexy as hell in jeans and a black T-shirt hugging his nicely cut arms and chest was none other than Travis Shepard.

"Well, I'm glad I stuck around," Carly said under her breath.

Savannah shushed her then moved toward the front of the store, aiming to put a barrier between Travis and her sister. Why was he here after she'd told him that she wanted to keep her search quiet? Had she made a colossal mistake trusting him?

"Hey," he said with a smile, as if nothing was out of the ordinary.

"Hi. Can I help you with something?"

Carly stepped up beside Savannah and propped her arm on Savannah's shoulder. "If she can't, I'd be happy to try."

Damn if Travis didn't gift Carly with a wide smile. "Depends on who can get me a peach pie to take home." He shifted his gaze to Savannah. "I hear you make the best peach pie in the county."

Carly sighed dramatically. "Foiled by my big sis's Betty Crocker genes."

Savannah looked over at her sister. "Don't you have somewhere you have to be?"

Carly just smiled, her unique brand of evil shining in her eyes. "Why are you trying to get rid of me?"

"Because I have a customer," Savannah said through gritted teeth.

Carly hesitated a moment, then winked at Savannah before she moved toward the front door. "Don't do anything I wouldn't do."

As the door closed behind Carly, Savannah shook her head. "I need to dunk her head in a tub of ice."

Travis laughed. "She's just like I remember her."

"A pain in my ass?" She sighed, then shifted her attention to Travis and lowered her voice even though they were the only two people in the building. "Why are you here? I told you that I didn't want anyone in my family to know about the investigation."

"I don't recall me saying anything about the search for your mother." He strode past her and started examining the contents of the store shelves. "Can't a guy just buy a pie?"

Savannah crossed her arms. "You're telling me that you drove all the way out here for a peach pie?"

"No, I drove out here for *your* peach pie."

"Travis."

He held up a hand. "Okay, fine, I have another reason. I had a case fall through this morning, so I thought if I could pick up the information about your mother, I'd jump right in."

"And you couldn't call to tell me that. We could have met anywhere but here, or I could have emailed you everything."

He slid a pie off the shelf. "But I can't get pie through the phone or email."

"Fine. Take a pie, take two. Stay here and I'll run up and get the information. Please, if anyone comes in…"

"Savannah, I meant what I said last night. I won't tell a soul."

She searched his eyes and saw truth looking back at her before she nodded and hurried toward her apartment. Her nerves were firing so much that she knocked over a glass of water on her coffee table and had to hurriedly grab the folder of information she'd gathered for him. After toweling up the water, she took a moment to try to get her frantic heartbeat under control. She wasn't used to feeling so out of sorts. But she didn't dare hesitate long. It would be just her luck for her father to come rolling in again and see through her deception in one glance.

When she returned to the store, Travis was sitting at

one of the tables, digging into a pie with one of the plastic forks from the front counter. Frantic to get him out of the store, off the ranch, back to Dallas, she hurried forward and placed the folder on the table beside his pie.

"Here you go."

He motioned toward the chair on the other side of the table with his fork. "Have a seat. I'll share my pie."

"It's too early for pie."

"It's never too early for pie."

"You need to leave."

Travis lowered his fork to the empty wedge in the pie tin where a slice of pie used to be. "Why are you so nervous?"

"I told you, I don't want my family to know I've hired you."

"They won't."

Throwing out her hands in frustration, she nevertheless sank onto the white metal chair. "My dad tracked me down on your phone. Do you honestly think he can't find out that you're a private investigator?"

"So what if he does?"

"How do I explain why I'm meeting with you?"

"He knows we went to high school together. Tell him that after we bumped into each other at the rodeo, we decided to hang out some."

"Hang out?"

"Yes. You know, friends do that from time to time." He leaned back in his chair. "In fact, I think we should hang out later tonight."

"You think you'll have some information by then?"

"It's possible but not likely. No, I was talking about going to do something fun that has nothing to do with your mom or any other member of your family."

Startled by his request, Savannah scrambled for a reason to decline. "I'm busy."

"Doing what?"

"Working."

He scanned the store. "What, do you work every waking hour?"

"It takes a lot to keep this store going, especially if I want to make the profits grow."

"You can afford one evening off."

"Why are you pressing this?" And why did she feel herself wanting to accept, even when she had no idea what he had in mind?

"Because you, Savannah Baron, are so stressed out that you look as if you're about to pop."

She opened her mouth to argue but found she couldn't. He was right. She'd never felt more stressed out in her life. Not even riding in the National Finals Rodeo had unnerved her as much as the past few days. She sighed and met his gaze.

"What did you have in mind?"

"County fair starts tonight. Ferris wheel rides, carnival games, funnel cakes."

She laughed a little and nodded toward the tin in front of him. "You're in the midst of eating a pie for breakfast and you're already talking about eating funnel cake. If you're not careful, you're going to wake up one morning and look like one of the elephants at the zoo."

"Don't worry about my figure. I have ways of keeping the weight off."

Heat rushed up Savannah's neck and into her face so quickly that she lowered her gaze before Travis somehow figured out where her mind had gone—right to the idea of him in bed, making love…to her.

She wondered if the lump in her breast was zapping

her brain, robbing her of common sense. Because why else would she be thinking about hopping into bed with Travis only days after seeing him again for the first time in years?

Because he was nice, funny and had a body that was made for exactly what she'd been imagining.

She couldn't believe that's where her mind went when she had so many more pressing matters to occupy her thoughts. But maybe that was exactly why she was imagining Travis that way, as a mental escape from her worries.

Travis picked up his fork again and cut a bite of pie. "So what do you say? Are we on for tonight?"

"If I say yes, will you leave?"

"Do you treat all of your customers this way, or am I special?"

Before she could respond, the front door opened and three women came inside.

Travis nodded toward the trio. "Go ahead and do your customer service thing. I'll just be here, eating my pie, waiting for an answer."

"Fine, I'll go." She stood and pasted on a friendly smile for the newcomers.

By the time she'd sold the ladies three pies, some jars of marmalade and one of the lace-covered picture frames she'd made, Travis still hadn't vacated the premises. Instead, he was wandering down one of the store aisles. Since obviously pressing him to leave didn't work, she simply stood at the end of the shelf and watched him.

"Don't tell me you have a burning desire to buy some craft items," she said.

"Just browsing. Rita's birthday is in a couple of weeks." He picked up the framed picture of a horse she'd made from scraps of cloth. "I bet she'd like this. Did you make it?"

"Yeah. I pretty much made everything in here, except the jewelry in the corner. Those are made by Gina, my assistant."

He glanced around the store at the variety of items on display. "Okay, so maybe you do work every waking moment."

"I like to stay busy, and I watch a lot of HGTV and haunt a lot of online crafting sites."

He grinned at her. "A woman of many talents. I'm impressed."

"I wish everyone felt the same way." What she wouldn't give to hear her father say one word of admiration for what she'd done with the store, turning it from a simple roadside stand into much more. But Brock Baron got things in his head a certain way, and changing his vision was akin to steering the *Titanic* into a U-turn.

The sound of more vehicles entering the parking lot drew her attention. Travis pulled out his wallet and handed over the money for the picture.

"I'll pick you up at six," he said, then headed toward the front door before she could think of a way to get out of spending the evening with him. She had a feeling steering clear of her family was the least of her concerns. Topping the list was eating funnel cake with Travis while pretending she hadn't imagined him naked.

TRAVIS WAS A couple of miles down the road before he realized he was still smiling. When he'd gotten up that morning, he'd had no intention of driving out to the Baron family ranch. But the next thing he knew, he'd turned the opposite way of his office and headed toward the slice of Texas that he'd called home in his youth. He'd told himself it was for business, but the truth was he'd wanted to see her again. He was a guy who figured out things, and what he wanted to figure out more than anything right now was Savannah Baron.

Why was she really looking for her mother? What besides the fear of her family finding out about her search was making her so anxious? And had he really seen a flicker of interest in her eyes as they'd sat across from each other in her store?

Since Corinne's death, he hadn't really dated, other than a blind date Rita had tricked him into. For a long time, he'd been too hurt, too angry. Then he'd just been too busy. That hadn't bothered him since he wasn't interested in finding someone else.

But when he'd run into Savannah, something unexpected inside him shifted and interest flickered to life. Was he nine kinds of a fool for even allowing himself to think the way he was? Could he perhaps casually date a little without letting himself get attached? Just a few friendly outings. By the time he found her mother and she got whatever answers she needed, maybe she'd be out of his system.

Blossom gave him a curious look as he finally made his way into the office around eleven o'clock.

"Look who finally deigned to show up. If we were having a late start today, I would have appreciated a call, a text, smoke signal even."

"You're just grumpy because you were out too late last night."

"And you're jealous because my life is more exciting than yours."

"Tell me why I put up with you again."

She smiled and batted her lashes. "Because I'm awesome at my job and keep things interesting around here."

"Oh, yeah, that." He laughed a little under his breath and walked into his office.

"Where were you anyway? I didn't have anything on your calendar for this morning."

"Went to see a friend."

He normally shared everything regarding cases with Blossom, but he said nothing about Savannah. She'd been so concerned about keeping her case private that at least for now he decided to keep it between the two of them. Not that he didn't trust Blossom, but he didn't want to give any sort of hint that he might be into Savannah. If there was anyone who could spot things people were hiding better than him, it was Blossom. He'd even offered to train her to become another investigator, but she'd wanted no part of it. She'd lifted a brow at him and said, "I can think of way better things to do with my nights than sitting in a car waiting to see some schmuck do the nasty with his piece on the side."

She had a point. Honestly, he could, too, but he went with what paid the bills. But not tonight. All the cheating spouses, insurance frauds and thieves would have to just wait another day to be caught because he had a date with cheesy carnival games, fat-laden foods and the prettiest cowgirl he'd ever seen.

THE CARNIVAL WAS a riot of sounds and smells. Screams from the roller coaster, game hawkers calling out the chance to win big prizes, the greasy scent of corn dogs and French fries. A couple of grinning kids walked by holding funnel cakes and with their mouths coated in confectioner's sugar. It all made Savannah feel ten years old again, let loose on the midway by her father with a string of tickets as long as she was tall.

Travis leaned close. "You're glad you came, aren't you?"

He seemed so happy with himself that she couldn't help but smile. "I admit it takes me back a bit."

She'd ridden in plenty of rodeos that were accompanied by carnivals, but she'd rarely taken the time to stroll through them. Her focus had been on posting fast times and then looking ahead to the next event. Since cutting back on riding, her focus had shifted to her new passion: the farm store and making sure the ranch produced the best and most peaches and pecans that it could. She liked having goals, a purpose, but she had to admit it was nice to get away from responsibility now and again, too. She just hoped tonight turned out better than her rodeo weekend in Mineral Wells.

Travis stopped at the cotton candy vendor and bought a big puff of pink sugar.

"I thought you were a man on a mission to have funnel cake."

He grinned at her and extended the cotton candy. "The night is young."

She shook her head. "Boy, you are on your way to a raging case of diabetes."

"Nah. You've only seen my naughty eating side."

Lord, the last thing she needed to think about was him having a naughty side.

"So, did the information I gave you help?"

Travis stopped and turned toward her. "You really want to talk business? We're here to have fun."

"What are we supposed to talk about?"

"About how I'm going to beat you at the shooting gallery?"

"What?"

Travis pointed to the right, at one of the game trucks that invited people willing to fork over hard-earned money to shoot toy guns at fake tin outlaws.

"You know those are rigged, right?"

"That's your excuse for not being able to beat me?"

Okay, he was just too cocky for his own good. She stared straight into his blue eyes and said, "You're on."

Before Travis could pull out his wallet, she strode up to the booth and handed the man the money required for both her and Travis then motioned toward one of the toy guns.

"Be my guest."

With a crooked grin, Travis picked up the gun, aimed and shot.

"And a miss," she said, humor in her voice.

Travis narrowed his eyes at her then aimed again. This time he hit the cartoon outlaw, knocking the tin cutout over. "That's more like it."

"Yeah, you're a regular sharpshooter."

His final three shots produced only one more hit, yielding him the amazing prize of a key chain with a little cowboy boot on the end.

Savannah couldn't help the snicker that escaped her.

Travis playfully bumped his shoulder into hers. "It's your turn, Annie Oakley."

Determined to back up her teasing, she aimed carefully at where her mind told her she should shoot then shifted slightly to the right to accommodate for what she expected was the rigging of the game. She pulled the trigger, and the tin outlaw fell backwards.

"Lucky shot," Travis muttered.

She smiled as she brought her eye to the sight again. Four more shots, four more fake outlaws toasted. She eyed Travis as she brought the barrel of the gun to her lips and blew on it as if there were actual smoke drifting from it.

The carnival worker manning the booth handed her a huge yellow teddy bear.

"I thought you said these games were rigged," Travis said as they walked away from the game.

"They are." She shrugged. "I'm just that good."

Over the next few minutes they wandered through the midway watching kids play games, finished off the cotton candy and ended up near the rides. Travis pointed at the roller coaster.

"Want to give it a whirl?"

"I don't think my bruised ribs would weather that very well."

"Probably not. Kiddie ride?" He pointed toward a miniature merry-go-round on which preschoolers were riding everything from elephants to dolphins, his expression and voice filled with humor.

She didn't know if it was a good idea, but she liked his teasing. It lightened the weight that had been sitting on her chest since the night of the rodeo.

"How about we compromise and go for the Ferris wheel?"

Savannah wondered at the wisdom of her suggestion, however, when she and Travis were seated close together in one of the passenger cars, his arm stretched out behind her. She stiffened at his proximity, which proved a bad decision when the wheel jerked into motion. A pain shot through her side, causing an involuntary grunt.

"You okay?" The concern in Travis's voice as well as the feel of his hand on her back sent an unfamiliar warmth through her.

She nodded and leaned forward as if to relieve her discomfort. Breaking contact with him should have allowed her to breathe easier, but she was left feeling an odd loss.

"How long does the doctor think it'll take you to heal?"

Her breath caught until she realized he was referring only to her bruised ribs. "A few weeks."

"So I guess you won't be competing anytime soon?"

"No. I was supposed to ride in New Mexico next month, but I already canceled."

"Guess you're not as crazy as the bull riders."

"It'd be a different story if I were in the hunt for the Finals. But I've had my fill of life on the road."

"But you can't give it up entirely?"

She shook her head. "It's in the blood."

This time when the wheel moved, it slid into motion more smoothly. There was something freeing about being up in the air, high above all the laughter, music and bright lights below. In the distance, she saw flickers of lightning.

"Looks like we're in for a storm later," Travis said beside her.

She nodded but didn't take her eyes off the horizon. For a moment, she allowed herself to wonder if her mother was out there somewhere, what she was doing, whether she ever thought of her children. Savannah pressed her eyes closed and shoved the thoughts away. She was having fun, and she didn't want it to end quite yet.

Tonight she would spend time with a good-looking man, allow herself to laugh and forget her cares. Tomorrow was soon enough to face the real world again.

Chapter Six

Halfway back to the ranch, it began to rain. The pace increased the closer they got, and by the time they made the turn onto the road that paralleled the ranch Savannah could barely see the road in front of them. Loud booms of thunder and bright flashes of lightning made Savannah jump several times.

"I'm surprised you could even see where to turn," she said.

"I would have probably missed it if we hadn't just passed that dead armadillo in the road. I saw it earlier."

"Navigating by roadkill. That's new."

Travis glanced at her and chuckled. In the next moment, they ran over something that made an unholy racket beneath the truck. Travis cursed and looked in the rearview mirror.

"Damn, I have no idea what that was."

Savannah hoped it hadn't been an animal, though thankfully it hadn't sounded like the distinctive thud that accompanied hitting a dog or cat. If they'd hit anything larger like a horse or cow, they wouldn't still be rolling down the road.

Somehow, Travis managed to spot a dirt pull-off beside the gate that led into Jackson Bennett's pasture. "I need to check what that was."

"It's pouring rain. If someone else comes along, they might not see you."

He turned on the SUV's flashers. "I'll be careful." And then he opened his door and jumped out into the downpour.

She didn't like the idea of him striding down the road when any other drivers couldn't see more than a couple feet in front of them, but she wasn't in a position to tell him no. Instead, she twisted in her seat and watched him until he disappeared into the dark deluge. She stared hard, as if that would somehow give her the ability to part the rain and see him. Her stomach twisted more the longer he was gone. But while she couldn't see him, she also didn't see any headlights piercing the night.

"Come on, come on," she said.

As if in answer to her plea, Travis appeared alongside the SUV, then jerked the door open and hopped in, looking more like a soaking wet river otter than a man. But then an otter wouldn't have a T-shirt sticking to its chest like a second skin.

Savannah snatched her gaze away from Travis's chest before he could notice. "What was it?"

Travis wiped rivulets of water from his face. "Two-by-four with nails poking out of it. No idea if I hit the nails." He turned off the emergency flashers and carefully pulled back out onto the road.

It wasn't long before it became apparent that they had indeed hit at least one of the nails. As Travis turned into the parking lot for the store, she heard the distinctive thwump-thwump of a tire going flat over the sound of the rain continuing to pound down.

"Bet you wish you hadn't taken me to the carnival now, don't you?"

"Are you kidding? I had funnel cake, a corn dog and

got soaked to my skin. That's exactly what I wanted when I woke up this morning."

Savannah laughed and shook her head. "You're just not right."

Travis shrugged. "I've had worse said about me. Funny how a guy doesn't like you when your report of his infidelity allows his wife to take him to the cleaners."

"You don't have any sympathy for them?"

"For cheaters? Not one bit. I figure if you're not happy in your marriage, get divorced. Then do whatever you want with whomever you want."

"I have a feeling you might be in the minority there."

"Maybe, but I had a good example. My parents are every bit as in love now as when they met forty years ago."

"That's sweet. You and Rita were very lucky."

"Yeah, we were. I'm sorry you didn't have that."

"Me, too." It wasn't that she thought her dad hadn't loved every one of his three wives, but it just wasn't the same as two people making a commitment and sticking to it for a lifetime.

Though she couldn't be too hard on her dad. After all, her mother had walked away from him as much as she had her children. And then he'd grieved Peggy's passing in his own way. Thankfully, despite their age difference, he and Julieta still seemed to be doing fine, helped by the fact that Julieta had a way of handling Brock that Savannah had never seen before.

Travis pulled out his phone and looked up the local weather radar. Even from where she sat, Savannah could see the endless wave of red and dark green marching across the phone's screen.

"That doesn't look like it's stopping anytime soon," she said.

"Nope. Good thing I'm already soaked."

"No changing the tire in this storm, not while it's lightning."

"It shouldn't take me long."

She fixed her gaze on him. "And it only takes a moment to get fried. Ask Juan, who works on the farm." She pointed out the windshield toward where the rows of peach trees were shrouded by the rain. "He was trying to finish up some picking before a storm a couple of years ago, and he got blasted right off the ladder he was on. Broke his arm and had burns on both his hands and feet. He couldn't work for two months."

Travis winced. "So maybe I'll wait."

She smiled. "Good idea." She glanced out the window and could barely see the front porch of the store with its collection of rocking chairs. "We might as well go in and wait for this to pass. I'll make some coffee."

"You'll get drenched."

She smiled at him again. "I have dry clothes inside." Savannah fished her keys out of her purse. She patted the large teddy bear she'd won, which had spent the trip back to the ranch sitting between them. "Looks as if you've got to sit here awhile, buddy."

With that, she hopped out into the driving rain. By the time she reached the cover of the porch only a few yards away, she was as wet as if she'd jumped in the pool up at the main house with all of her clothes on.

As she slid her key into the lock, Travis bounded onto the porch behind her.

"We're going to leave puddles all the way through the store," he said.

"That's what mops are for."

Soaked as they were, the cold of the air-conditioning inside hit Savannah like a wintry blast. She rubbed her arms as she shut and locked the door then headed toward the back stairs that led up to her apartment.

"That coffee sounds even better now," Travis said as he followed her up the steps.

Too late, Savannah realized that perhaps inviting Travis into her home wasn't the best idea she'd ever had. On a normal day, her apartment had plenty of room. But add one tall, good-looking guy, and it shrank substantially. She crossed the open living area and placed the kitchen counter between herself and Travis. Without making eye contact, she started filling the coffeemaker with grounds and set it to brewing.

When she did look back across the apartment, Travis hadn't moved from the spot right next to the door.

"What are you doing?"

He pointed at the rug below his feet. "I don't want to get your floor wet."

She waved him toward one of the iron bar stools on the opposite side of the counter. "The floor will be fine." A little water wasn't going to hurt the coated pine.

Savannah wouldn't have thought it possible, but the hammering of the rain on her roof increased. "Grab the remote and flick on the TV."

Travis complied. As she expected, the Dallas weather guy was in full swing talking about the storms.

"We've had reports of wind damage coming out of Plano tonight and multiple instances of flash flooding. What we're most concerned with right now is this area right here." He pointed at what any Texan with a TV knew was a bow echo, an indicator of a potential tornado either forming or on the ground. "If you're in this line north of Fort Worth, take cover immediately. Most in danger right now are Boonsville, Cottondale and Boyd."

The meteorologist panned back on the map to show

the string of almost uninterrupted storms lined up all the way back to the New Mexico border.

"Somebody did something to tick off Mother Nature," Travis said.

And there was no way she could send Travis out into that mess. She mentally argued with the thought that popped into her head and barely kept it from flying out of her mouth. But as she turned her back to Travis to pour two cups of coffee, the weather report didn't magically get any better. If anything, it sounded as if things might get worse. She closed her eyes and told herself not to get so freaked out. She could be an adult about this. Travis was her friend. She'd shelter Abby just the same.

Yeah, but Abby didn't make her think inappropriate thoughts.

Savannah grabbed both cups of coffee and turned around, extending Travis's toward him.

"Thanks," he said as he accepted the mug and wrapped his hands around it for a moment before taking a drink.

She took a slow sip before setting her cup on the counter. "I'm going to see if I have anything dry you can wear."

"No sense in that. I'm just going to get soaked again."

"Nope, you're not." She pointed toward the couch. "Because you're going to sleep right there."

Travis lifted a brow.

She nodded toward the TV. "If you go out in that, you're likely to run off the road. And I need you to not kill yourself being an idiot too stubborn to wait out a storm."

The edge of his mouth quirked up. "You certainly know how to boost a guy's ego."

"Most guys I know don't need any boosts to their egos." She headed toward the bedroom, telling herself she needed to stop thinking about how attractive Travis was and remember he wasn't interested in anything remotely romantic.

When she closed her bedroom door behind her, she was able to breathe a bit easier. Had she really just invited Travis to spend the night? Granted, she'd made it clear he'd be sleeping on the couch, but still. She'd never done anything like this before. And after being so anxious about having anyone in her family see him at the ranch, what kind of sense did it make for her to tell him he was not only staying longer but also overnight?

Well, if anyone said anything, she'd explain it simply as it was. He had a flat tire, the storm was raging outside and she didn't want to risk him having an accident on the way home. Anyone with any compassion would understand that. They didn't have to know that she was probably going to lie in bed all night staring at the ceiling, unable to relax because Travis was sleeping only a few feet away.

Oh, for Pete's sake, get a grip on yourself.

It wasn't as if she hadn't ever spent the night with a guy under the same roof. She just didn't do it at the ranch. For someone who had been married three times, her dad could still be old-fashioned when it came to his kids, especially his daughters. Even her brothers had been known to be a touch overprotective, so she found it easier to keep her relationships far from their prying eyes.

Not that any of that had anything to do with Travis.

Savannah moved away from the door and started digging around in the bottom drawer of her dresser. If she remembered correctly, there was a pair of sweats Jet left behind when he'd held down the fort at the store one weekend when she was away riding in a rodeo. When she finally found the pants, she paired them with the largest T-shirt she owned, one that swallowed her but that would probably be tight on Travis. At least it was dry. She tried not to think about how it would probably mold to his body. Just glancing at how that wet, black T-shirt he was wearing now hugged his muscles had nearly had her sticking her head out into the rain to cool off.

And if Carly or Abby knew what was in Savannah's head now, she'd never, ever hear the end of it.

She tossed the shirt and sweatpants on the bed while she changed out of her own wet clothing. As she slid on clean underwear, she realized that was the one article of clothing she couldn't provide for Travis. He'd either have to wear what he had on or…no, she did not need to think about him going commando.

"Savannah Baron, you are an idiot," she whispered to herself.

With a shake of her head she crossed to the door and pulled it open as if nothing out of the ordinary was going on, as if she had guys sleeping over all the time. She handed him the shirt and pants.

"Bathroom's through there." She pointed toward the door. Another door opened off the side of the bathroom into her bedroom. She'd have to remember to close it tonight.

"Thanks."

Her breath caught when his hand grazed hers as he took the clothes, and she wasn't quick enough to hide her reaction. Also, before she could think better of it, she looked up into his eyes. Yep, he'd noticed how that simple touch had affected her. The only thing she could do was pretend her ass off.

She stepped away and headed toward the kitchen. "How about I make us something real to eat?"

"I'll have you know that fair food is a recognized food group."

"Yes, recognized by cardiologists everywhere."

Travis laughed, and damned if she didn't like the sound of that male rumble filling her space. Maybe the intensity of her focus on work at the expense of a love life hadn't been the best idea after all. She didn't draw a full breath until he disappeared into the bathroom. For several seconds, she just stared at the closed door, wondering what Abby or Carly would do in this situation.

Dumb question. They'd march right over to the door, open it and join him. Savannah had to say the idea was enticing, but she couldn't in a million lifetimes imagine herself doing it, not with someone she'd known since she was little more than a kid.

Needing to focus on something besides the thought of Travis naked, she pulled some grilled chicken and stir-fry vegetables from the freezer and tossed it all in her wok along with the necessary seasonings, then started a small pot of brown rice. Her mouth watered at the idea of something remotely healthy passing her lips. Beginning with the peach muffin she'd had that morning, all the way through the fair food, she'd had nothing but junk all day. Her body was on the verge of rebelling. She was supposed to be healing, and she doubted a corn dog or cotton candy was on the get-well menu.

When Travis exited the bathroom holding his pile of wet clothes, she used the spatula to point toward the laundry room. "Put them on top of the washing machine, and I'll do a load in a minute."

"You don't have to do my laundry, Savannah."

"I'm going to be washing mine anyway. What's a couple more things?"

Though she told herself not to look, she caught herself glancing at Travis as he walked toward the laundry room. Just as she'd predicted, the shirt was snug. But it was the sight of his bare feet that for some reason sent shivers racing across her skin. Okay, she didn't have a foot fetish, so what was up with that? Maybe it was nothing more than the fact that he was walking around her apartment with body parts uncovered that normally weren't. That she thought he looked right at home, and she didn't mind it.

Yeah, she was cracked.

"That smells good."

She glanced over to see Travis leaning against her refrigerator. "I know it's not a deep-fried hunk of dough, but it'll have to do."

"So, you take in sodden motorists often?"

"Oh, yeah, all the time. You'd be surprised what an excellent revenue stream it is."

"You can pitch that to your dad, the Baron B and B."

"Um, no." If her dad had his knickers in a twist about the viability of the store, she could only imagine his reaction to a bed-and-breakfast. He wasn't a B and B sort of guy.

Travis took a couple of steps toward her, and she'd swear she heard "Danger, danger, Will Robinson" in her head, even though he hadn't given her any vibe other than friendship. No, she was the one she didn't trust. So what did she do? She shoved the spatula at him.

"Keep stirring this while I start the laundry."

As she hurried to her bedroom to pick up her wet clothing, then carried it to the laundry room, she wondered if Travis was thinking he'd agreed to spend the night in the home of a crazy woman. He might be right.

Resolving to act casual and normal when she returned to the kitchen, she started the water running into the washing machine and added the detergent. She could do this. All she had to do was focus on the fact that Travis was simply someone she'd hired to do a job. She'd allowed herself to forget that tonight, and that decision had led her thoughts down a path that had her jumping every time he even came near her.

It wasn't just because he was a guy. After all, she didn't act like a skittish colt around Ben, Juan or any of the other ranch workers. Or around any of the cowboys on the rodeo circuit, not even when she would readily acknowledge there were good reasons the buckle bunnies chased them. What was it about Travis? Was it just that he was nice to her, that he wasn't expecting anything other than rekindling their friendship?

No, it was something else, and she'd felt it the moment they'd crossed paths at the rodeo. She'd never felt such a powerful attraction before, and it had hit her when she least expected it. Add in the fact that Travis was totally the wrong person to be attracted to, and she wanted to curse the storm for putting her in her current awkward situation.

After all, her past relationships had been casual and short-lived, something she couldn't imagine with Travis. He was the kind of guy who got married, loved his wife completely and mourned her loss years later. She had a hard time seeing herself in that serious of a relationship, though she'd never wondered why. Had watching her father lose not one but two wives scarred her somehow?

Shaking off her attempt at self-diagnosis, she realized the washing machine was already half-full of water. She tossed her clothes in followed by Travis's. When she grabbed for the last item, she halted her hand just before touching it. A pair of black boxer briefs lay there atop the dryer, taunting her with the knowledge that the man currently tending the stir-fry wasn't wearing any underwear.

Her body flooded with warmth as she threw the briefs into the wash and slammed the lid a little too forcefully.

"You okay?" Travis called out.

"Yeah, lid slipped."

Remembering her resolve from a minute before, she straightened, took a confident breath and returned to the kitchen.

"I think it's done," Travis said.

She pointed toward one of the cabinets. "Grab a couple of plates out of there, please." When he handed them to her, one at a time, she loaded them up with food.

"Looks as good as it smells," Travis said as he accepted his plate.

"What's important is how it tastes."

He scooped up a bite and uttered an "mmm" of appreciation. "Even better."

She couldn't remember the last time she'd cooked for a man who wasn't related to her, and she had to admit it was nice to receive the compliment. Her own plate in hand, she headed for the couch so she could use watching the weather report as a buffer between her and Travis. It really was ridiculous how nervous he made her.

When Travis plopped down on the couch, too, she could have kicked herself for not choosing her chair instead.

It's okay, silly. There's plenty of space between you.

She focused on the TV so intently that when a huge boom of thunder sounded like an explosion right above her living room, she yelped. She glanced toward the window. "Holy crap on a cracker."

"It keeps this up all night and I don't think either of us is going to get any sleep."

It had to be her imagination, totally her imagination. Because Travis couldn't be thinking what she was—that there were other reasons for not getting any sleep. When she dared a glance his direction, he was focused on the TV. Yep, totally her imagination. The storm wasn't going to be the reason she wouldn't get any sleep.

She did her best to focus on the weather report and finished eating her stir-fry. Once her plate was empty, she grabbed Travis's, as well, and headed toward the kitchen.

"You want more?" she asked from a safer distance.

"No, I'm stuffed. Thank you."

See, that was a nice, normal thing to say. Good, just go forward from that. She rinsed the plates and forks and stuck them in the dishwasher. After pouring herself another cup of coffee, she grabbed her laptop and headed for the big, cushy chair this time. She propped her feet up on the ottoman and turned on her computer.

"Back to work mode?" Travis asked as he stretched out on the couch facing her.

"Just checking email." As soon as the words came out of her mouth, she realized that hiding behind her computer was the chicken route. Not to mention rude. So she closed the screen and set the computer aside. "Sorry. I just tend to slip into my routine."

"And I knocked you off your routine tonight."

"It's okay. I had a nice time."

"I'm glad. You seemed stressed."

She fidgeted with a seam on the chair's arm. "Yeah. Always lots of work to do."

"I don't think it was work that had you so on edge."

"It's enough, but add on beginning this search for my mom and keeping it secret and it's stressful."

"You haven't talked to your sisters or Jet about this?"

"No."

"Why not?"

She hadn't prepared for that question, so she stumbled. "Because…I don't want to disappoint them if I find nothing."

Travis shook his head where it lay against one of her quilted pillows. "That's not it."

"You're calling me a liar?"

Travis lifted to his elbow. "*Lie* is too harsh a word. Fib, maybe."

She shifted her gaze to the TV screen where the weather guy was now talking about another area of concern farther west.

"Savannah, you can trust me. It won't leave this room."

In that moment, the weight of her secret and the worry she'd been carrying around like a gigantic knot in her stomach were too much to handle alone. The need to talk to someone overrode her determination to keep everything to herself. And her secret thoughts about Travis's scrumptiousness aside, she realized he was offering to be the kind of friend she needed right now.

She exhaled a shuddery breath. "Everything I told you was true, but I don't know if I would have ever taken the first step toward looking for my mom if I hadn't fallen the other night."

Travis's forehead creased. "I don't see the connection."

"After you brought me back to Abby's trailer, I got in the shower. While examining the damage, I…I found a lump in my breast. When I had it checked Monday, the doctor asked if I had any family history of breast cancer and I realized I had no idea."

Travis sat up slowly. "But you're okay, right?" The tense concern in his voice touched her deeper than it should have.

She blinked against tears that felt sudden but which had been building since her fingers had accidentally found a little lump that had the potential to change her life. Maybe even end it.

No, she couldn't think that way.

She held the tears at bay as she met his eyes. "I have no idea."

And that was the scariest thing of all.

Chapter Seven

Travis prided himself on being intuitive. It's what made him good at his job. But despite the fact that he'd pressed Savannah to tell him the real reason behind the search for her mother, he hadn't predicted what her answer might be. Even if he had, he wouldn't have come up with what she'd just said.

He fought the urge to retreat, to run through the rain and sleep in his truck. Since losing Corinne, he'd steered wide around anything that hinted at death. He was only able to perform investigations involving someone's passing because he didn't know the person.

But he knew Savannah, liked her and hated the idea of her facing a grim diagnosis. "Most times it's nothing, right?" He desperately needed it to be nothing, mostly for her sake but, selfish as it might be, also for his. If he was going to be working with her, he didn't want to think about the possibility of her having cancer every time he looked at her.

"Sometimes."

She sounded so very alone. "Why tell me instead of one of your sisters?"

"I don't want to worry anyone without cause, especially Lizzie in her condition. And like you said, it could be nothing."

"Does the doctor have to know if cancer is in your family history?"

"No, but it made me realize that I have no idea what other things might be lurking there. And not just that. I barely know anything about that branch of my family. And…let's just say I have a lot of unanswered questions."

He wanted to promise her that he would find her mother, but he couldn't know that. What he could promise was that he'd try his best. If he focused on the search, maybe he could avoid thinking about her health. "I'll turn over every stone I can find."

A wan smile tugged at her mouth. "Thank you. Did you have a chance to look through everything I gave you?"

"Most of it, but I'll go through everything more carefully when I get to the office tomorrow and devise a plan of attack."

"I'd like to be kept up-to-date with each step."

He nodded. Normally, he would give reports every week or so, but Savannah wasn't just a normal client. He'd like to be able to say that his willingness to talk to her more frequently had nothing to do with the first stirrings of attraction he'd felt since Corinne, but he couldn't. There was something about Savannah's combination of strength and vulnerability, her dedicated work ethic that managed not to sacrifice her ability to have fun that drew him.

She was so different than Corinne and yet she was the first woman who'd held his interest since the loss of his wife. Part of him felt a twinge of guilt, but then Rita's words rang in his head. Corinne wouldn't have wanted him to be alone, even though it felt wrong to be thinking about moving on.

Why did he have to be attracted to someone who could possibly be facing a fight for her life? He sighed. He might not be able to help the attraction, but he didn't have to act on it.

Savannah shifted her attention to the TV, but her expression told him that her thoughts were elsewhere.

"You look tired. Go get some rest." He motioned toward the angry radar image on the TV. "I'll be up for a while, so I'll keep an eye on things."

"I am beat, but I don't want to be rude."

"You're not. It's not as if you were expecting company."

Even after she acknowledged that she needed to go to bed, she didn't move. He knew that feeling, as if she was contemplating just curling up in the chair to sleep so she didn't have to expend the energy to walk into her bedroom.

He stood and crossed to the chair, then extended his hand to her. "Come on, up you go."

After a moment, she lifted her hand and placed it in his. When he wrapped her hand in his, he liked the feel of it. Though smaller, it wasn't dainty. And she had the calluses that came from working on a ranch, from handling saddles and ropes. Even so, her touch was unmistakably feminine. Despite her fatigue, there was strength there, too.

Travis tugged her to her feet, resisting the sudden urge to pull her all the way into his arms. But then he remembered what she'd said about that lump, and he released her instead. It had absolutely nothing to do with her breast and everything to do with how he ached at the idea of losing anyone else he cared about. Even though it was unreasonable to think he'd be able to live the rest of his life without losing anyone, he didn't have to invite it.

"There's a quilt on the back of the couch, fresh towels in the cabinet in the bathroom. If you get hungry or thirsty, just help yourself to whatever you can find. Need anything else, let me know."

"I'll be fine. But do you mind if I use your computer?"

She nodded toward the laptop. "Go ahead."

He didn't reach for the computer until Savannah closed her bedroom door. Even then, he stood listening to her move around, wondering if she was changing into pajamas. Or did she wear a nightgown? Old T-shirt? Nothing?

At that thought, even the borrowed sweatpants grew a little uncomfortable. With a growl of frustration, he snatched up the computer and sank back down onto the couch. He might be stuck here for the night, but he could make good use of the time and start his search for Delia Baron. First things first: find out if she was even using the same name anymore, and if she was still alive. He hoped she was because the last thing Savannah needed right now was the news that her mother was dead.

After a couple of hours, not even the last of the coffee and walking around her apartment was able to keep his eyes from drooping. But when he pulled off the too-tight T-shirt, turned off the TV and lamp and stretched out on the couch, his thoughts drifted toward the woman in the other room.

Was she asleep? Or was the fact that he was in her space preventing her from getting the rest she needed? As if her bruised ribs weren't enough, now she had to concern herself with that lump. What he wouldn't give to be able to just take it from her, but in that area he was powerless. He could, however, help her get something else she needed—answers and maybe even some closure. What she didn't need right now was a guy panting after her. And he didn't need to be the one doing the panting.

SAVANNAH HAD NO idea what time she finally fell asleep, but she'd still been awake when the light in the living room went out. She'd had to fight the urge to walk out there and ask if he'd been working on her case, if he'd found anything. She'd had to tell herself morning was soon enough to get the answer to that question. Besides, it wasn't as if they were going to go out and track down her mother in the middle of the night in a barrage of storms.

So she forced herself to close her eyes and listen to the rain on the roof, which had lessened in intensity. At some point she'd drifted off and awakened a few minutes before five. Her body was just used to waking at that time. She was as quiet as she could be as she showered and dressed for the day. By the time she exited her bedroom, gray dawn light was filtering in through the windows.

Only a couple of steps into the living room, Savannah caught sight of Travis on the couch and froze. He was sprawled as if he didn't have a care in the world, his bare chest on full display. Damn if her mouth didn't water, and it wasn't because she was hungry for breakfast. Her fingers itched to run across that smooth flesh, up from his taut stomach over the nicely defined pectoral muscles. She knew she should stop staring, but she couldn't. She'd never get this chance again.

When Travis grunted and shifted, she jumped and nearly yelped in surprise. Before she allowed herself to get caught ogling, she headed downstairs to start the morning's baking. Maybe if she buried herself in work, she'd forget the half-naked guy upstairs.

Ha. No amount of baked goods would be able to push the image of Travis Shepard's bare chest out of her thoughts.

As she pulled out pans and the ingredients for peach muffins, she glanced at the clock. She told herself to chill when she thought about someone getting wind that he'd spent the night. After all, there was a perfectly reasonable explanation. And if her father or even Lizzie made the connection between the fact he was a P.I. and Savannah asking questions about her mother? She'd just say it was a coincidence. Those happened all the time, right?

She was putting the first batch of muffins in the oven ten minutes later when she heard footsteps upstairs. Immediately, she wondered if he was walking around shirtless. The image was so burned into her brain that when he descended the stairs, she was almost afraid to turn around. Calling herself an idiot for thinking Travis would stroll into her store with his chest on full display, she glanced over her shoulder.

"Good morning."

He mumbled something that might have been a reciprocal "good morning" but could have been a hundred other responses, as well.

Savannah chuckled. "Not a fan of early mornings, I take it."

"This is prime sleeping time," he said as he made a beeline for the fresh pot of coffee on the counter beside her.

He filled the largest takeout cup she had, then appeared to down half of it in one gulp. As he stood there with his eyes closed, it seemed as if he were waiting for the caffeine to perform its magic.

Savannah thought about her question from the night before, if he'd found out anything about her mom, but refrained from asking him in the interest of him vacating the premises.

Travis took another drink of his coffee. Then, as if he sensed her anxiety building, he said, "Well, I better tackle that tire."

All she could manage was a nod.

"I'll call you with a report later today."

"Sounds good."

She glanced at him as he turned and headed toward the front door. Once again unable to pull her gaze away, she watched him, appreciating the way he moved.

Wait, he was wearing his clothes from the night before. She'd been so tired and out of sorts when she'd gone to bed that she'd forgotten to toss the laundry in the dryer, so he must have. The idea of him seeing her bra and panties made her blush like a silly teenage girl.

She was still appreciating his backside when he opened the door to reveal Carly. Savannah stared as her sister's mouth curved into a wide grin full of mischief. Just great.

"Well, hello there," Carly said. "We meet again."

"Morning, Carly."

Her sister looked beyond Travis, straight at Savannah. "You start opening for business earlier, sis?"

Savannah's mouth opened to speak, but nothing came out. Her brain screamed at her to say something, anything, like the truth, but instead she probably looked like a fish lying on the shore gasping.

"I had to bum your sister's couch last night. I ran over something in the storm and had a flat." Travis pointed toward his vehicle, but Carly kept her eyes on the two of them.

"I hope she was a good host."

Savannah was so going to kill Carly.

"She was. Now to tackle this tire and get to work." Travis glanced back at Savannah and lifted his cup. "Thanks for the coffee." And then he winked.

An unexpected thrill went through her at that most likely innocent gesture. She'd bet he was just trying to say, "Your secret is safe with me," or "I did the best I could steering your sister clear of her obvious assumption." Still, she had to fight a giddy smile because that was the last thing she needed to show Carly right now. Or Travis.

Once Travis descended the porch steps, Carly turned and shot him an appreciative look that probably was an exact copy of how Savannah had been watching him moments earlier. She didn't like it, not one bit. But instead of saying that, she returned to rolling out dough for turnovers.

She loved her sister dearly, but she wished Carly would leave without another word. Of course, she wasn't that lucky. Instead, Carly shut the door and strolled back to the kitchen.

"Well, well, well," she said. "Had a boy-girl sleepover, huh?"

"You can just stop dreaming up scenarios because they'd all be wrong."

"What am I thinking? That there's no way you had that delicious man in your apartment all night and didn't attack him? I couldn't believe it when I figured out it was Travis Shepard."

Savannah sighed and shifted her gaze on her sister. "We went to the fair last night, and on the way back we drove into the first of the storms. He ran over a board with nails in it that probably blew off somebody's barn in all that wind. By the time we got here, the tire was almost completely flat."

"And he didn't have a spare?"

Savannah propped her hand on her hip. "Pardon me for thinking that it wasn't a good idea to change a tire in a downpour with the sky filled with lightning. I didn't want him to get fried like Juan."

Carly's expression changed to one of grudging acceptance. "So nothing?"

"Nothing."

"Did they check your eyesight at the hospital?"

Savannah wadded up a dish towel and pitched it at her sister. "We're just friends, you twit."

"Uh-huh."

"Why are you here so early anyway?"

"Needed to get away from the house. Decided to go for a ride before it gets too hot."

Which all sounded plausible except that Savannah suspected more was going on than Carly was saying.

"Early ride, huh? So that means you probably have plans for later." Carly was a barrel racer, too, but she also liked to go out with friends and have a good time. Rarely did a day go by when her sister didn't have something that took her out and about.

"I might."

Savannah didn't ask. After all, she didn't want Carly prying into her business.

"And you're getting your ride in by standing in my store how?"

"Girl's got to check on the safety of her big sis when she sees a strange vehicle outside her front door."

Savannah wasn't fooled. "You knew exactly whose SUV that was."

"Okay, I wanted to see if you were getting a little something. So sue me."

Savannah spun and charged her sister, making Carly squeal and race out of her reach to relative safety on the opposite side of the display case. The movement reminded Savannah that she was only a few days out from having fallen off a horse.

"You okay?"

"I will be if I can get back to work, unless you want to stay and help."

Carly curled her lip. "No, thanks." She propped her

arms against the top of the case. "Take my advice and tackle that man the next time you get the chance."

"Goodbye, Carly."

With a chuckle, her sister headed toward the front door. "I'm not blind, sis."

Why couldn't Travis have left before anyone saw him? Oh, well, that boat had sailed, and she had no doubt that before the end of the day the whole dang ranch would know about her overnight guest.

AFTER GETTING THE tire changed and going home to shower and change clothes, Travis finally made it to his office only to be greeted with the raised eyebrows of his office manager. Choosing to ignore her inquisitive look did him no good as Blossom simply followed him into his office and plopped down in a chair before he even had a chance to sit in his.

"Okay, out with it," she said.

"Out with what?"

"Really? You're going with the whole 'I don't know what you're talking about' play?"

He sank into his chair and leaned back with his hands behind his head. "What do you think is going on?"

"You've either got a client you're not telling me about or a secret girlfriend."

"I still think you should train to be my assistant."

"So which is it?"

Knowing she wasn't going to let this go, he sat forward, his arms on his desk. There wasn't really a reason to not tell Blossom about the search for Savannah's mom. After all, Savannah had hired his firm, and Blossom was part of that firm. Telling her wasn't the same as sharing Savannah's secret with anyone else. And maybe Blossom could help. "New case, but it's for a friend."

"Oh, tell me it's not another cheating spouse. I'm beginning to despair that marriage is a dying institution."

Travis barked out a laugh. "You're interested in marriage?"

"Not right now, but I'd still like it to be a viable option if I ever find Mr. Right."

"O-kay. Did you get hit in the head by something in the storms last night?"

She snarled at him. "You suck."

He laughed as he opened a desk drawer and pulled out the folder containing the information about Savannah's mother. "No, it's not a cheating case. My friend's mother walked away from her family when Savannah was a little girl, and she wants to know why."

Blossom shook her head. "Why do people do that? Have kids and then abandon them?"

"That's what I need to find out. But first I have to find her."

"Tell me what I can do."

"Check the DMV, other public records for a Delia Baron."

"Baron? As in Baron Energies?"

"Yes, thus the need to keep this quiet."

"Who would I tell? Besides, you know me better than that."

"Yes, I do."

"So, this Savannah? She more than a friend?"

"Nope, just a friend." As much as he loved and trusted Blossom, he wasn't going to share the kinds of thoughts he'd been having about Savannah. Ones that had kicked into high gear the night before when he'd tossed the laundry into the dryer and spotted her lacy bra.

For some reason the look of that soft, dainty fabric had surprised him. Savannah had always tended more toward the tomboy end of the female spectrum, even though she'd been beautiful no matter what she wore. He hadn't expected her to be the type of woman who wore matching underwear sprinkled with little pink flowers and edged with lace. Standing there in her small laundry room, he'd gone rock-hard.

Just the memory threatened to put him in the same state again.

"A girl can hope."

Blossom's words drew his attention away from the increasing discomfort in his pants. "What's that supposed to mean?"

"That maybe it's time you did find someone again."

"It's not that simple."

"Finding the right person never is. Take it from someone who hasn't even gotten a whiff of hers yet."

"I've already been down that road."

At this, Blossom set aside her normal snark, instead wearing a serious expression. "I know, and the road was much too short. But that's the thing about life. There are lots of roads to travel, lots of them with pretty scenery it would be a shame to never see." With that she rapped her knuckles on the top of his desk once and headed out to her space to get to work.

Travis didn't know if he agreed with her, but he at least appreciated the fact that she wasn't one of those women who felt the need to hound something to death. She spoke her mind then moved on.

He opened the folder and spread all the materials Savannah had given him out across his desk. He needed to bury his mind in work so he didn't sit there fantasizing until he got hit with a permanent erection.

He had to keep reminding himself of that countless times over the next week as he followed a string of dead ends in the case and kept having inappropriate thoughts about Savannah.

But why were they inappropriate? She was single, beautiful, a good person. And he was beginning to think maybe Blossom was right and it was time to move on. He still thought about Corinne every day, probably always would. But no matter how much he might wish otherwise, she was gone. And he hopefully still had a lot of years left to live.

But what about Savannah? Was her demise already growing inside her?

He shook his head. No, early detection was key. Modern medicine could do amazing things now. She would be okay, and he suddenly accepted the fact that just talking to her on the phone about the case wasn't enough. He picked up the phone and dialed her number, suddenly as jittery as he'd been the day he'd finally gotten up the nerve to ask Corinne out the first time.

"Peach Pit, how can I help you?"

"Hey, Savannah."

"Oh, hi. Can you hang on a minute?"

"Sure." He listened as she set the phone down and talked to someone, probably a customer. But the longer he had to wait, the more he fidgeted.

"Sorry about that," she said when she came back on the line. "Was with a customer."

"I figured."

"I just got my first order for a wedding cake. The bride is from Georgia originally, so they're having a peaches and longhorn themed wedding."

Not knowing what else to say to that, he said, "Congratulations."

"Thanks. Do you have something new?"

"I was wondering if you'd like to go out to dinner tonight?"

"Sure, where and what time?"

She obviously thought this was a business meeting he was proposing.

"This has nothing to do with the search for your mom." He let that sink in for a moment before continuing. "I'm asking you out on a date."

"Oh."

He had to smile at the surprise in her voice. For someone as pretty, talented and as well-off as she was, it was endearing how being asked out on a date evidently hadn't even crossed her mind. Of course, he'd given her no reason to expect that was coming.

"What do you say?"

"I…I don't know."

For a moment, he wondered if he was making a mistake. But then he shook off his doubt and plowed forward. "I have an idea. Say yes."

She hesitated for a moment. "Okay."

Smiling again, he said. "I'll pick you up at six."

"Wouldn't it be easier for me to meet you somewhere?"

"Maybe, but it's not a proper date unless the guy picks up the girl."

When they ended the call a few moments later, he leaned back in his chair. That's when he realized his door was wide-open and Blossom was standing in the doorway wearing a huge grin and giving him two thumbs-up.

"I knew it!"

He pitched one of those squishy stress balls at her, but she dodged out of the way and out of view. "You're fired."

"No, I'm not. You need me too much."

Drat, she was right. And he didn't care, because he had a date with the prettiest girl in Texas.

Chapter Eight

As Savannah placed the phone back in its base, she couldn't decide if she was excited or scared out of her mind. Or maybe both.

"You okay?" Gina asked as she came back in from taking out the trash.

"Yeah."

"You sure? Because you look like you just stuck your finger in an electrical socket."

"I just got asked out on a date."

"Your friend Travis?"

Savannah looked at Gina. "How'd you know?"

"Well, that wasn't much of a stretch. He calls every day, and Sierra Phillips saw you two at the fair the other night and said you looked as if you were having fun. I figured that was a date, especially since he's already spent the night."

"Crap. And here I was hoping Carly had kept her mouth shut." She shook her head. "It wasn't a date, and he slept on the couch because it was too dangerous for him to change his tire and drive home in those storms."

"Well, whatever happened before, looks as if he's upping the ante now, doesn't it?"

Yeah, he was, much to her surprise. And that realization set loose a storm of butterflies in her stomach. Those butterflies multiplied in number as the day progressed. Not even work or talking with customers alleviated the riot happening in her middle. By the time she went upstairs to shower and change, she thought she might toss her cookies.

When she found herself staring into her closet, she realized she had no idea what to wear. Where were they going anyway? Surely he wouldn't drive all the way out to the ranch to pick her up only to return to Dallas, would he?

After finally settling on jeans and a blue, sleeveless top, she pulled her hair up into a ponytail and applied a minimal amount of makeup. She wanted to look nice but not as if she was trying too hard in case things went no further than the one date. Why had he suddenly changed his mind anyway? The night of the rodeo, she'd been sure he wasn't interested in dating. He wasn't doing this just because she'd told him about the lump, was he? If she'd had to lay down money, she would have bet on that revelation sending him running in the opposite direction. If this was a pity date, she didn't want it.

A couple of minutes before six, she heard him pull up outside. She forced herself to take a slow, deep breath then let it out just as slowly before heading downstairs. Thankfully, no one was around this time, no smart-ass sisters or overprotective father lurking on the front porch.

Savannah was glad to see Travis was dressed casually as well in jeans and a soft-looking gray T-shirt. And damn if he didn't look great, so much so that she feared the butterflies in her stomach were going to suddenly break free.

When they made eye contact, she could only manage one word. "Hey."

"Hey, yourself."

His smile drew a reciprocal one from her. –

He nodded to her right. "I see he's made himself at home."

She looked at the bear she'd won at the fair, which she'd dressed in a Peach Pit T-shirt and sat in one of the rocking chairs. "He likes the view."

Her words faded away, leaving what felt like a yawning silence.

"I need to know something," she said.

"Okay."

"This isn't a pity date, is it?"

His forehead furrowed in confusion.

"You know, because of the whole lump thing."

A flicker of something in his eyes made her wonder if she'd just made him reconsider asking her out. But then he met and held her gaze.

"No." He didn't elaborate, and the fact that he didn't caused her butterflies to return.

"Oh."

Travis leaned back against the front of his vehicle. "Are you as nervous as I am?"

Shaky laughter bubbled up out of her. "Yes."

"Crazy, isn't it? We've known each other for years. And we already went to the fair together, so we know we'll have a good time."

She loved how he was being so open and honest, and the thought flitted through her head that Travis was different from every other guy she'd dated. In fact, she suddenly wanted their date to go really well. Though that pressure should have made her more nervous, he'd succeeded in alleviating her anxiety.

"So where are we going?"

"It's a surprise."

She tried to imagine what he might have up his sleeve over the next thirty minutes, but she hadn't even gotten close. He'd turned off the highway and taken a gravel road. If she hadn't known him for years, she might be a little worried. But as they came through a line of red oak trees, her mouth dropped open in surprise. Spread out across a field were several hot-air balloons, some flat on the ground and others in various stages of being filled with gas.

"I'm going to guess by the look on your face that this was a good idea."

She glanced at Travis. "What in the world?"

"There's a race tomorrow, so they're doing test runs tonight," he said. "A buddy of mine is out here somewhere."

"He has a balloon?"

"Yeah. Evan was a fighter pilot until he got injured. Though he can still see well enough, his injuries prevented him from ever flying an airplane again. So he took up ballooning when he got over being angry."

"That's good that he found another way to enjoy flying." She scanned the field, taking in the bright colors and designs on the large balloons. "I've never seen a hot-air balloon up close."

Travis pulled his SUV into an empty spot in the field and parked. "Then today's your lucky day."

She glanced at him again. Yeah, it was, and a lot of that had nothing to do with balloons.

They got out of the vehicle, and she followed him as he weaved his way through the balloons. As they approached a fully inflated balloon with alternating blue-and-yellow vertical stripes, the guy next to it looked up and waved.

"Hey, you made it," the lanky blond guy said.

The man and Travis shook hands. "Good to see you." Travis glanced at her. "I'd like you to meet Savannah Baron. Savannah, this is Evan Black."

Evan shook her hand and smiled, then shifted his gaze

back to Travis. "You didn't tell me you were bringing a beauty queen."

Savannah laughed. "You didn't tell me he was as full of hot air as his balloon."

Evan smiled even wider. "I like her, even if she is mistaken. You, my dear, are gorgeous."

For someone who recently maintained she didn't have time for a man in her life, she certainly was enjoying all the attention.

Evan, who reminded her a bit of Slider in *Top Gun,* one of her favorite older movies, looked at Travis. "You ready to go up?"

"In the balloon?" she asked.

"Yeah, I convinced this knucklehead to let us do a tethered ride. You up for it?"

"Are you kidding? It's one of the things on my bucket list."

A satisfied smile settled on Travis's lips. "Am I good or what?"

"What, I'm the one with the balloon. Maybe I should take her up," Evan said.

Travis playfully slugged his friend in the arm. Something about that action woke a very feminine part of her, a part she hadn't even known existed but that liked having a guy establish with another that she was off-limits. Travis wasn't being a brute or domineering about it, but there was definitely something sexy about his simple actions. Coupled with the fact of where he'd taken her on their first official date, and she was glad she'd said yes when he asked her. This was much better than watching HGTV, eating alone and worrying about her health and if they'd find her mom.

After a feinted punch back at Travis, Evan opened the door on the wicker basket and gestured for Savannah to board. Travis joined her and Evan released several of the weighted bags until the balloon started to slowly rise.

Savannah gripped the edge of the basket and scanned the ground below. Dozens of balloons stretched out in all directions, a rainbow of colors and designs. There was even one that was University of Texas orange and shaped like a longhorn, complete with horn extensions. As they rose higher, she could see beyond the trees to the highway. She glanced over her shoulder to look to the south. Ranch land dotted with cattle extended off to the horizon.

"This is amazing." She'd flown numerous times, had marveled at how tiny everything looked from a plane. But this was different. She could inhale the early evening air, feel the sun warm her face, bask in the remarkable sense of freedom. "I can totally see why people take up ballooning."

"Yeah, I didn't expect to like it the first time Evan took me up, but it surprised me."

"It's as if your cares float away on the breeze."

"Then I'm glad I brought you."

Savannah turned to face Travis. "I am, too. Thank you."

They spent a few minutes pointing out various balloons, impressed by the artistry of some and laughing at others, such as the one that was shaped like a giant pig.

"I guess pigs do fly," Savannah said and laughed.

"It actually makes me hungry. What do you think of barbecue when we get down from here?"

"Sounds good."

Savannah hated to see the ride end, even though all they did was float in one spot. But Evan needed to secure the balloon for the night.

When the basket settled back on the ground and Savannah stepped out, she looked up at Evan. "Thank you. That was awesome."

"Maybe I'll take you for a real ride sometime."

"And maybe you won't," Travis said, a knowing smirk on his face. "This guy left a trail of broken hearts from boot camp to Afghanistan back to Texas."

"I've not had any complaints."

Travis snorted. "Just keep telling yourself that."

After saying their goodbyes, Travis and Savannah walked back to his vehicle and headed in search of barbecue. They ended up at a little place on a country road called Amos's Barbecue Shack. It looked like little more than the shack spelled out in its name, but judging by the number of trucks in the parking lot they must serve up some mean barbecue.

Inside, it was wall-to-wall people, but they were lucky to find one table open, a mini booth that had room for only one person on each side. Even among the crowd, it felt tucked away and oddly private.

A cute young waitress with bobbed black hair streaked with electric-blue came up to the table with an order pad in hand. "Hey, I'm Wendy. What'll y'all have?"

"What's good?" Travis asked.

"Everything, but Amos is the king of barbecued ribs. And we have a special tonight on the endless rib basket for two."

"Sounds good."

Savannah scanned the menu. "Sounds messy."

"All the best food is messy," Travis said as he tipped her menu down with his forefinger.

She dropped the menu onto the table. "You know, you're right."

Travis smiled as if he'd just won a bet and was looking

forward to collecting his winnings. "One basket of ribs, it is. And I'll have a Shiner."

"Lemonade for me," Savannah said.

When Wendy headed for the kitchen with their order, Savannah scanned the rest of the restaurant. Her gaze settled on the big guy on the other side of the order window. She nodded toward him. "He looks as if he could be a professional wrestler."

"He was. That's Amos Tucker."

"I thought we happened upon this place by accident."

Travis shot her a gotcha grin. "There's a method to my meandering."

"You planned all this just since I talked to you earlier?"

"What can I say? I'm a man who can get things done."

Just like that, her thoughts veered off toward their professional relationship. "I know we're supposed to have fun tonight, but what's the latest with the search?"

"We talk about this until the food gets here, and that's it for the night, okay?"

She nodded. "Deal."

Travis leaned his forearms on the table. "I haven't found any current records for her, no driver's license, deeds, anything like that. It's possible she changed her name, or that she doesn't live in Texas anymore."

Savannah swallowed against the lump forming in her throat. "Or she could be dead."

Travis slid his hand across the table and clasped hers. "Don't jump to that conclusion. We've only begun to scratch the surface. There are other places I can look, and I have some queries out. These things sometimes take time, especially if a person doesn't want to be found."

"Hard to believe a mother would hide from her own children, isn't it?"

"Honestly, in this job I've seen just about everything. Nothing really surprises me anymore."

"But you like it."

He shrugged. "I'm good at it. I suppose it's like any other job. There arc good days and ones where you wish you could win the lottery and retire to the beach and fish your life away."

Wendy made a quick reappearance with their drinks before hurrying off to refill the glasses of a large party a few tables away.

"What about you?" Travis asked. "How did you end up working at the family farm?"

"Sort of fell into it. I was helping out at the roadside stand one day when I mentioned I wanted to cut back on how much I was traveling to rodeos. Luke, the ranch manager, said he could use some help with the farm part of the operation, the peach and pecan crops. I already knew the land and what we grew backward and forward. And it kept me away from Baron Energies."

"Makes sense. I can't picture you working in an office."

"No, that's Lizzie's area. I'd go completely crazy."

"You said you had plans for the store. What are they?"

He couldn't know how much it meant to have someone ask about her vision for the Peach Pit and seem genuinely interested. It touched her deeper than was probably wise.

"Gina and I produce pretty much everything now, but I'd like to devote a section to area craftspeople, people with a lot more talent than me. Continue to create new peach- and pecan-flavored bakery items, start a mail-order side to the business. Maybe even have tours of the farm, something that would bring in people by the busload and really make the venture profitable."

"You should develop an agritourism plan and incorporate school groups into it. Evan's brother has a farm in Tennessee, and school groups have been a huge addition to his bottom line, especially in the fall. They have a pumpkin patch, hayrides, a corn maze, all kinds of stuff that the kids love."

"That's a great idea. Of course, we'd have to adjust it to our crops somehow."

"You could host some sort of farm festival for the community."

Excitement coursing through her veins, she pulled the small pad and pen from her purse and started jotting down all the ideas. "We could have a peach and pecan bake-off, a trail ride, dunking booth, roping lessons."

"Cowboy poetry."

She wrote that down, too.

Travis chuckled. "I was kidding on that last one."

"No, it's a good idea. It's actually very popular. Jet's even tried his hand at it."

"Maybe I should start P.I. poetry."

She wrinkled her nose at that.

"Okay, maybe not."

Savannah was still writing down ideas as fast as she could when Wendy returned with a huge basket of ribs, a tub of coleslaw and another of potato salad.

"Oh, my God. That looks like an entire cow."

Wendy laughed at Savannah's assessment. "No one ever goes away from Amos's hungry."

After Wendy zipped away again, Savannah continued to stare at the mound of ribs for a few seconds, then lifted her gaze to Travis's. "You're going to have to roll me out of here in a wheelbarrow."

As soon as she sank her teeth into the first rib, Savannah made a sound of appreciation. "I'm never eating barbecue anywhere else again."

Travis grinned at her. "Maybe you can convince Amos to cater your festival."

"Don't tempt me. Only we'll have to have a rule that everyone buys all their desserts from the Peach Pit first. They won't have any room left afterward."

Despite Travis's bragging that he'd still have room for some blackberry cobbler when the ribs were gone, they only managed to eat half of them and a third of the two side dishes.

Savannah raised a mocking eyebrow at Travis as he leaned back in the booth with his hand on his stomach. "And he goes down in defeat."

"I admit it. I feel like if I eat one more rib I'll sprout horns and start mooing."

Savannah wiped the barbecue sauce from her fingers and glanced at the long list of ideas they'd brainstormed. "Thanks for this."

"Was nothing. Just tossing out any crazy thing that came into my head."

"Well, it means a lot to me."

"You already had a good foundation there. Sounds as if you've set the Peach Pit on the right path to growth."

Savannah sighed. "I wish my dad could see what you do. Sometimes I wonder why I try so hard. It seems like no matter what I do with the store, he can't see what is right in front of him."

"Of course not. It's your vision, not his. Not to mention he's a stubborn old coot."

Savannah laughed. "That he is."

"You'll just have to prove him wrong."

Travis sounded so matter-of-fact, as if Savannah's eventual success were a given, that something shifted inside of her. She was pretty sure it was her heart, and that she just fell a little in love with Travis. No one had ever accepted her vision as if it made perfect sense, as if he could see her dream realized as easily as he could see Amos Tucker dishing up countless baskets of ribs.

Movement at the front door drew her attention. "Crap."

"What?" Travis looked over his shoulder.

"Yes, that would be my brothers who just walked in."

Travis turned his gaze back to her. "It's okay. We're just two friends out having barbecue."

She wanted to thank Travis for understanding, but Daniel and Jacob had already spotted them and were headed their way.

"Hey, Savannah," Jacob said. "Fancy seeing you here." He shifted his attention to Travis. "With a date."

"And this is noteworthy?"

"Just didn't know you were seeing anyone."

"I wasn't aware I had to run it by the entire family first."

Travis leaned his forearms on the table. "Savannah and I ran into each other recently and decided to get together and catch up. It'd been years."

Savannah admired how smoothly Travis had given that explanation without a hint that their night out was anything other than two old friends swapping tales about high school classmates. She supposed being smooth with half-truths would come in handy with his job.

"You should come over to the ranch sometime," Daniel said. "We can all catch up."

"Maybe I will."

Jacob eyed the table next to them, as if willing the family sitting there to leave. But considering they'd just received their food, he was out of luck, thank goodness.

"You should try the ribs tonight," Travis said. "They're good. Hope you brought a big appetite though."

After another moment, Jacob nodded. "Well, we better nab a table."

Once Jacob and Daniel were out of earshot, she met Travis's gaze. "Please ignore my hovering brothers."

Travis shrugged. "Don't worry about it."

She breathed a sigh of relief, glad to be away from Jacob's and Daniel's watchful eyes, as she and Travis left the restaurant a few minutes later.

She wanted to recapture the warm feeling that had flickered to life in her chest at their little booth prior to her brothers' arrival. But as Travis drove her home, she sensed a change in him. He was quieter, more distant. Her brothers might not have meant to put a damper on her date, but they had. Still, the closer they came to the ranch, the more she didn't want the night to end.

As he parked in front of the Peach Pit, she tried to think of something to say that would extend the evening by even a few minutes. "We made it back without any flat tires or crazy storms. I guess that's a step up."

"Yes, but that means I still have an hour to drive home."

Was he hinting that he wanted to come inside? Savannah had to admit that part of her wanted that very much, but she also knew she wasn't ready to take that big of a step, especially after the run-in with Daniel and Jacob. Even if you counted her and Travis's outing to the fair, they'd only been out twice.

She didn't know what name to put on her feelings for Travis, but they were definitely more than professional or casual friends. But she didn't know what the right move was at this point. She was used to casual dates, not ones that felt like…well, not exactly casual.

"Sorry about that," she finally said when she realized she hadn't responded.

He gifted her with a small smile. "No apology necessary. I had a good time."

"Me, too." Great, in fact. The quiet grew awkward, and she opened her door. "Good night, Travis." She hopped out of the vehicle and headed for the porch before she could do something crazy like invite him to spend the night, and not on her couch this time. She already had too much on her mind. She didn't need to add a serious relationship to the mix.

Her heart rate jumped into a higher gear when she heard Travis's door shut behind her just as she reached the top of the porch steps.

"Savannah?"

She turned and watched him walk slowly toward her, still looking too good to be true in the dim light. "Yeah?"

"You going to let me take you out again sometime?" There was something in his expression, almost as if his thoughts were warring with each other, the ones prompting him to ask her out again barely winning.

"Maybe." Damn if her voice didn't crack a little.

The wooden steps creaked as he climbed one, then two, putting himself eye to eye with her. "I guess that's better than a no."

She smiled a little and realized her butterflies had returned with a vengeance. "Be careful on your way home, okay?"

"Will do."

She turned and headed for the door, but a voice inside her head started screaming at her to turn around, to not let him go. Not allowing the time to talk herself out of it, she changed directions yet again and crossed to Travis. She framed his face with her palms and brought her lips to his.

A solitary moment passed, probably as he processed the shock, maybe considered pulling away, before his arms came around her waist and tugged her close. As he deepened the kiss, his warm, firm lips taking more full possession of hers, her hands slid to the back of his neck. When he parted her lips and slid his tongue inside, she couldn't prevent the sound of pleasure that escaped her. Travis reciprocated with a groan of his own and slid his hand up her back, leaving a scorching trail in its wake.

Savannah knew she should pull away, but the will to do so evaded her. Being held like this, kissed as if she were the last woman on earth, felt so good that she could stay there on the porch steps in Travis's arms forever. But they eventually needed to breathe, and Travis was the one to break the kiss and take a step back.

"I think you should go inside, Savannah."

Her heart stuttered in her chest. Had she just made a huge mistake? Had she misread his interest? No, how he'd kissed her said otherwise.

Travis caressed her cheek. "Don't worry. Everything's fine."

"Okay." She wasn't able to disguise the doubt in her voice.

His thumb grazed her bottom lip. "The only reason I'm pulling away is because right now I want more than kissing. And if I'm reading you correctly, you're not ready for that. I'm not sure I am, either, despite what my body is telling me."

Her eyes widened. "Oh."

He smiled at her. "Yeah, oh."

Savannah took a step back, breaking contact. "Uh, well, good night then."

"Good night."

This time when she reached the door, she actually unlocked it and slipped inside, not allowing herself to look back at Travis. Because if she did, she wasn't entirely sure they wouldn't end up right where both of their thoughts had already taken them.

Chapter Nine

Travis didn't move until he saw the light flick on in Savannah's upstairs apartment. Even then he stood in the same spot for a few more moments, half believing that he'd imagined the kiss. The first kiss he'd given a woman since the last time he'd held Corinne in his arms before shipping out to Afghanistan.

Finally, he forced himself down the steps and back to his vehicle. When he was in the driver's seat, he looked up at the lighted windows, hoping to catch a glimpse of Savannah. But not even a shadow showed through the blinds. With a deep breath, he started the engine and headed home.

As the miles ticked by, he couldn't shake the feeling of having been hit by a stun gun. The moment Savannah's lips had touched his, he'd felt it all the way down to his toes. Even as much as he'd loved Corinne, he'd never experienced anything that intense with her. And that made him feel as if he really was betraying her.

Corinne had loved him, but she'd died alone with him thousands of miles away on the other side of the world. For all he knew, he could have been shooting hoops or telling dirty jokes with the guys at the moment she'd taken her last breath. It felt like the ultimate betrayal to think what was between him and Savannah was more powerful after one real date and one hot kiss.

He ran his hand over his face, trying to wipe away the guilt.

It wasn't Savannah's fault. She'd tried to walk away, but he'd followed her hoping for exactly what had happened. Well, not exactly. He'd hoped for a kiss, all right, but not one that shook him to his core, one that dredged up memories he tried so hard to not let rule him anymore.

Part of him whispered that he'd done nothing wrong, that he wasn't betraying Corinne because she was gone. But no matter what that voice inside him said, he couldn't fully banish the guilt. He'd eventually gotten to the point where he could function, even learned to smile again, have fun and reclaim his life. But there had been nothing even approaching a serious date. And if that kiss tonight was any indication, things were very, very different with Savannah.

Could he allow himself to feel that deeply for someone again? To risk the pain of losing her? He didn't think he'd survive it again. In fact, he was sure he wouldn't. Next time, he doubted there'd be enough of him left to pick up and start over. He wouldn't want to.

As much as he wanted to continue seeing Savannah, he needed to take a step back. Maybe the infatuation with her would fade if he just shifted his focus. It wasn't as if she was his only client. Tomorrow, he would work on other cases while he waited to hear back from the people he'd contacted regarding her mother.

He kept telling himself he'd made the right decision all the way home. But as he lay in his bed hours later, unable to sleep, he wondered if he could stay away. It would have been hard enough before the kiss. But now that he knew how her lips tasted, as sweet as the peaches she worked with every day? It was going to be damn near impossible.

SAVANNAH STOOD FROM where she'd been sitting on the floor rearranging a shelf of peach preserves. She hurried around the front counter toward the ringing phone, hoping it was Travis. She didn't know why she was torturing herself, because obviously her kiss was enough to send men fleeing.

It'd been three days since she'd seen him. After he'd left her with her heart beating out of her chest, she hadn't heard from him. Not unless you counted the text he'd sent the next morning saying he had to go out of town on another case and that he'd let her know if he found out anything else about her mother's whereabouts.

She grabbed the phone without even looking at the caller ID. "Peach Pit. How can I help you?"

"May I speak to Savannah Baron?"

"That's me."

"This is Susan from Dr. Fisher's office. We got your test results back, and Dr. Fisher would like to schedule you for a biopsy."

Savannah grabbed the edge of the metal prep table to steady herself when she grew lightheaded. "So it's cancer?"

"Not necessarily. Dr. Fisher needs to take another look to determine that. How soon can you come in?"

"How soon can I?" She couldn't stand waiting any longer to know if she had a clean bill of health or if she was in for a fight for her life.

"We actually just had a cancellation for tomorrow, so can you be here at nine?"

"Yes."

"Come to the same front desk as you did before, and they'll direct you to the right place."

"Okay, thank you." It felt so weird to thank someone for the opportunity to have a needle stuck into her breast.

After she hung up the phone, she felt as if all the blood had drained from her body, leaving her weak and dizzy. She managed to make her way to the steps leading up to her apartment without collapsing and sank down on them. She pressed her hand against her forehead and made herself take several slow, deep breaths until the worst of the dizziness subsided.

The burden of the knowledge of what was going on in her body weighed down on her, and she yearned to be able to relieve that pressure. She still didn't want to share the news with her family, but she could call Abby. But her friend needed to stay focused on riding and maintaining her points lead. Savannah knew Abby well enough to realize she would rush to Savannah's side and turn into a mother hen, hurting her chances of staying atop the standings.

She wished she could tell Travis, but he'd made it clear he didn't want to talk to her. How had everything in her life gotten turned upside down so quickly?

With work still to do, she should get up and back to it. But she couldn't find the energy, not even when someone stepped through the front door. For the first time since she'd opened the Peach Pit as more than a mere roadside stand, she wished the customers would stay away, give her this one day to process, to withdraw into a protective cocoon.

"Savannah?"

She jerked her gaze up and saw Travis looking back at her from the other side of the front counter. She blinked a few times, wondering if her mind had manufactured him. But no, he was still there.

"Are you okay?" he asked.

"Yeah, just tired."

His forehead creased in what looked like concern. Did she dare hope that she'd been wrong about his lack of feeling for her?

When he looked as if he might come around the counter toward her, she stood and returned to where she'd been working before the phone call. She hoped he didn't notice that her hands shook as she organized the last few jars of preserves. Without looking at him, she moved farther down the shelves and straightened the mini pecan pies even though they didn't need it.

"How did your other case go?" Only when she heard the skepticism in her voice did she realize that part of her had considered his explanation for his whereabouts had been a lie to avoid seeing her.

"Fine. It's over now. I had to testify at a trial in Austin."

She glanced at him and didn't see any deception in his eyes. Then she felt bad for thinking him a liar.

"But I'm here because of your case."

"Oh?" She fidgeted with the peach pies down on the next shelf.

"I may have a lead."

She stopped her busywork and turned toward him. "You found her?"

He held up a hand. "Don't get too excited. It's a possible first step in tracking her movements after she left here. I got a hit on her name, from about six months after she left. I've made some calls, waiting to hear back."

Savannah's heart rate sped up at the news. "Where was it?"

"Up in Oklahoma."

"So what now, do we go there?"

"Not yet. Lots of these potential leads don't pan out, so that's why I put in a call to someone I know in Oklahoma City. If we get something more concrete, then we reexamine."

So it was a tenuous lead, but it was a lead nonetheless. It was more than she'd had five minutes ago.

Travis leaned his forearm against the end of the shelf. "I also wanted to tell you that I'm sorry for not calling."

Trying to act as if it didn't matter, she shrugged. "You were busy. So was I."

"I thought we might go riding tomorrow."

She shook her head. "I can't."

"Gina could watch the store for a while, couldn't she? Or draft Carly."

"I have a doctor's appointment early in the morning."

"Oh." Travis hesitated before saying more. "Follow-up on your injury?" She detected a note of hope in his voice, and it broke her heart a little.

"No. I have to have a biopsy on the lump to see if it's cancer." She bit her lip when saying the words out loud brought tears to her eyes.

In the next moment, Travis was beside her, surprising her by enveloping her in his arms. She sank into the warmth of his embrace, needing his strength. She'd always been strong, independent, but this was different. She'd never had to face the fact that her body might be plotting against her.

"You'll be okay," he said, then planted a kiss atop her head. He sounded as if he was trying to convince himself as much as her.

SAVANNAH HEARD THE first bird chirp of the morning before any hint of dawn was even lightening the eastern horizon. Despite Travis's assurances that she'd be okay and her own attempts at giving herself pep talks, worry had settled on her like a cold, steady rain. She'd worked until the wee hours, hoping to get so tired that she'd fall asleep as soon as she hit her pillow. But even though she'd been exhausted when she'd trudged to bed, sleep remained elusive. She'd tossed and turned, stared at first the ceiling then out the window at the sliver of moon, trying to will herself to sleep. A warm glass of milk hadn't helped. Neither had music. Altogether, she'd gotten a grand total of maybe fifteen minutes of subpar sleep.

Yeah, that was a great way to go to the doctor, worn-out and cranky.

Tired of the fruitless search for rest, she got up and headed for the kitchen. If she couldn't sleep, she supposed the next best thing was to fully wake up instead of feeling like a zombie. She might as well make use of her time and finish the Christmas tree art made from green and red buttons.

Two cups of coffee and the rest of the buttons later, she held up the gold-fabric-covered canvas and admired the button tree. She liked it so much that she decided she was going to keep it for herself instead of putting it in the store. She wasn't feeling up to putting more energy into the store anyway. All the ideas she and Travis had come up with while eating barbecue ribs were still sitting unrealized on the notepad in her purse.

Hating how down she felt, so unlike herself, she pulled out the notepad and ran her fingertip over all the suggestions. A flood of determination filled her. After she was done with this biopsy, she was coming home and tackling one item on this list. If she had cancer, she would fight it tooth and nail. If not, she'd thank God, fate, her lucky stars, and never take life for granted ever again. But either way, she was going to move forward with her plans for making the Peach Pit a destination not to be missed by anyone visiting Texas. She would prove to her father that she was every bit as capable of being a business success story as he was.

He should know that when she put her mind to something, she kept working at it until she succeeded. She'd been that way with barrel racing from a young age, with her grades in school, and had already grown the Peach Pit far beyond what anyone had expected. But she wasn't finished, not by a long shot. And the stupid lump in her breast wasn't going to get in the way of her plans, even if she had to chop the whole thing off. She'd do it, recover and deal with life in the aftermath. It was better than moping about it or not having a life at all.

With a new, proactive outlook, she showered, got dressed and headed downstairs. She left a note for Gina that she had business to attend to in Dallas and didn't know what time she'd be back. Her bases covered, she headed outside.

Of all the things she could have encountered as she stepped out the front door, Travis was what she least expected.

"What are you doing here?" she asked.

"I'm taking you to your appointment."

"I'm perfectly capable of driving myself to Dallas."

He hooked his thumbs in the front pockets of his jeans. "But you shouldn't have to go through this alone."

That hit her right in the heart. She couldn't imagine anyone she'd ever dated before offering to accompany her to a breast biopsy, especially not someone who was so obviously bothered by the idea that something very bad could be happening in her body. It struck her how brave his being there truly was. "You don't have to do that."

"I know, but I'm going to."

She glanced at her vehicle. "I need to drive in so there aren't questions. I told Gina I had business in Dallas today."

"Where is the doctor's office?"

When she told him, he nodded. "My place is on the way. You can leave your car there."

"Okay."

She followed Travis all the way to the outskirts of Dallas, down a nicely shaded street full of houses built before everyone thought they should have at least three thousand square feet. She liked these smaller homes with their neatly kept lawns and pretty flower beds better than the subdivisions full of homes that would have been called mansions in another era. Yes, she'd grown up in a large, very nice home, but she honestly preferred her little apartment. It fit her personality more.

Travis finally pulled up in front of a small brick home. She had to smile because compared to some of the other houses on the street, this one screamed bachelor. The front porch was bare of any furniture, and the flower beds were empty save for a large rosebush at one corner of the house and some daffodils that had lost their bright yellow petals. She got the feeling this was not the home he'd shared with Corinne, and she understood why he likely hadn't wanted to live in their shared space anymore. Too many memories.

He got out of his vehicle and motioned for her to pull into the driveway. When she stepped out, he was there to greet her.

Travis nodded toward the modest house. "Home sweet home."

"I like it."

He laughed a little, as if he suspected she might be stretching the truth a little.

"Okay, so maybe it could use a little bit of personality."

"Yeah, I should plunk a statue of Sherlock Holmes down in the front yard." He extended his arms and simulated the plunking down of said statue.

"P.I. humor. Who knew?"

He smiled and turned back toward his vehicle at the curb.

It wasn't until she was buckled into the passenger seat and Travis had pulled out onto the street that she started to get nervous. Her new positive outlook threatened to abandon her. As if sensing her change in mood, Travis reached over and took her hand in his. He could have given her a quick squeeze of reassurance, but instead he entwined his fingers with hers.

Savannah looked across at him and smiled. "Thank you."

All he did was nod, but it was enough. In that moment, she felt even closer to him than she had when they'd kissed. She'd swear her heart expanded in her chest, filling with a depth of feeling for him that she was afraid to label.

Travis didn't let go until they had to get out of the SUV at the clinic. And even though she detected hesitation in him, he walked beside her as she headed toward the front door. He placed his hand at the small of her back as they stepped inside and up to the registration desk. And he stayed beside her, lending silent support, as she filled out paperwork and waited to be called back.

Savannah fought the urge to fidget as her appointment time approached. She actually jumped when Travis clasped her hand in his.

"It'll be over before you know it."

But as she watched her appointment time come and go,

her stomach rolled more and more. Finally, at the point when she was seriously considering running out the front door and pretending nothing was wrong, a nurse came out and called her name.

Savannah froze, suddenly very afraid of what lay beyond the door behind the nurse.

Travis squeezed her hand, drawing her attention. He lifted her hand to his lips and kissed it. "You're strong. You can do this."

Drawing on his confidence, she stood and took a deep breath just as the nurse called her name a second time. Her legs shaky, she followed the older woman. As Savannah passed through the doorway, she glanced back over her shoulder to find Travis watching her with an encouraging smile. She hoped this biopsy resulted in good news because she was definitely beginning to fall for Travis Shepard.

THE MOMENT THE door closed behind Savannah, Travis had to get outside to some fresh air. He'd been as supportive as he could for her, but he couldn't stand the sterile smell anymore. He'd felt the same way when he'd taken her to the hospital. It was part of the reason he'd gone to the Burger Barn to buy her some dinner.

Though Corinne had died well before they'd wheeled her into the emergency room, and he hadn't even been there, for some reason he still equated medical facilities with her loss. They always brought up those memories, making them as raw as they'd been when he'd stepped off the plane at Fort Hood knowing his wife was gone.

He had no idea how long Savannah would be, but he figured he could stay outside for a while, make some calls to see if he could chase down any more information about her mother. He walked away from where a couple of people were smoking but stayed within view of the lobby where he'd been sitting with Savannah.

Fifteen minutes later, he cursed under his breath as the lead he'd had on Delia fell through. He didn't look forward to telling Savannah that, and he decided that today was not the day to do so. What would it hurt to wait until tomorrow? Savannah certainly had enough on her mind without piling on a dead end in the search for her mother. He wanted to give her answers, not more questions.

Maybe he was going at the case all wrong. Perhaps if he figured out the reason why Delia left, then that might give him some sort of insight into where she might have gone. He put in a call to a law enforcement contact to see if he could dig up any allegations of domestic abuse. Even as cranky as Brock could get, Travis didn't think that was the reason for Delia's disappearance. Savannah had been old enough to remember if her parents were fighting, and she hadn't indicated that had been the case. Granted, they might have hidden it from her, so he needed to try to find out one way or the other.

When he exhausted what he could do while standing outside a medical clinic, he forced himself back inside. He didn't want Savannah coming out and seeing him gone. With two TVs tuned to different programs at opposite ends of the waiting room, one to a cartoon he didn't recognize and the other to one of those awful daytime talk shows, he went straight to the small alcove in the middle. It held four chairs and provided at least some buffer from the noise. The magazine selection was crap, so he resorted to playing games on his phone.

After what seemed like enough time for an entire generation to be born and grow to adulthood, but really wasn't more than an hour, the door next to the registration desk opened and out walked Savannah.

Travis hopped up from his chair and crossed to her. "You okay?"

"Yeah, nothing an ice pack and some ibuprofen won't help."

"And ice cream," he said as the perfect idea popped into his head.

"I wouldn't argue with that."

When they reached his SUV, he opened the door for her and attempted to help her in.

"I'm okay. What's a little needle in the boob?"

He laughed, glad to see at least most of her anxiety from earlier had dissipated. Waiting was always the worst part of anything you were dreading, but, of course, now she'd have to wait for the results. If he could will a good outcome, he would. But as it was, he'd have to wait and wonder the same as her. He really wanted her to be okay, and he hoped he had the strength to be there for her even if she wasn't.

Travis backed away from her and swallowed the lump that appeared in his throat. He could not allow himself to think of that possibility because he didn't like the image of himself running away to avoid losing someone again, of how easily he could imagine himself giving in to the temptation to do exactly that. It was easier to face down enemy combatants in a foreign land than to look that kind of loss in the eye.

When they passed by a grocery store a few minutes later, Savannah pointed at the shopping center. "You know you just passed the store, right?"

"Yep. This isn't just an 'any ice cream will do' kind of day."

"It's not? Because I think there was probably some Häagen-Dazs back there with my name on it."

He glanced across at her. "I've got something better in mind."

"Better than Häagen-Dazs? This I've got to see."

She winced a little as she adjusted what he assumed was an ice pack under her arm.

Five minutes later, he pulled into one of the parking spaces at Ed's Dairy Drive-In. A quick glance at the bright look in Savannah's eyes, and he knew he'd made the right choice.

"I can't believe this place is still open. I haven't been here in years."

"You remember the time a bunch of us decided to invade after that basketball game?"

"Oh, my God, yes. It was homecoming senior year, and there were, what, sixty or so of us who skipped the dance and descended on Ed's instead? I think we freaked the poor employees out."

"What I remember is Amber Carmichael dumping a strawberry milkshake on top of Josh Freeman's head after she found out that he'd cheated on her with Shannon Denton."

Savannah lifted her hand to her mouth and laughed. "You know, I secretly loved that. Amber was a bitch."

This time he laughed. "True."

"Welcome to Ed's," said a female voice over the speaker. "What can I get you today?"

Travis looked to Savannah. With a grin, she said, "Strawberry milkshake."

They both started laughing, probably making the gal inside think they'd lost their marbles. But Travis didn't care. It was good to see Savannah looking happy.

After they got over their laughing fit, they managed to claim their order of cheese fries, hot dogs, the hilarity-inducing milkshake and a banana split then headed for his house. After parking, he grabbed all the food except for her milkshake.

"I'm not going to end up wearing that, am I?" he asked.

She pursed her lips as if considering his question. "I don't know. Do you deserve to wear a milkshake?"

"Me? I'm an angel."

"Pfftt," she said, then opened her door.

When he slipped from the driver's seat, it was to find Savannah standing behind his SUV.

"Thanks for going with me today," she said. "I appreciate it."

"No problem. Glad to do it."

She reached for the bags he held. "Sorry to run, but if I can get my food, I'll head home."

He shook his head. "Oh, no, you don't." He nodded toward the house. "You're going in, eating your lunch and relaxing for the rest of the day."

"It wasn't that big of a deal. I should get back to work." The wince as she glanced over at him belied her words.

"Humor me."

He got the feeling the anesthetic was just beginning to wear off because she didn't argue any further, allowing him to escort her into his house and to the couch.

"Don't you have to go to work?" she asked.

He pulled their food out of the bag and set it all out on the coffee table. "That's the beauty of being your own boss. No one to tell you when you can and can't work."

"But you have to work to make money."

"It'll still be there to make tomorrow."

As they ate, they reminisced about other classmates and where everyone was now.

"I heard Robbie Dearborn moved to L.A., went into acting," she said.

Travis nearly choked on a cheese fry. "You could call

it that." At Savannah's curious look, he continued. "Let's just say you're not going to see any trailers on TV for his movies."

"Bad, B-rated stuff?"

"More like X-rated."

Savannah's eyes widened. "No way!"

"Yes way."

"Oh, my God! I cannot wait to tell Lizzie. She had the biggest crush on him. She will just die of embarrassment."

As they finished their food, he noticed fatigue beginning to tug on Savannah's eyelids. "You look tired."

She yawned as if to emphasize his observation. "I barely slept a wink last night."

He stood and grabbed the blanket off the back of the couch. "Stretch out for a bit and rest."

She made as if to stand. "I need to get home."

He gently pushed her back down on the couch. "I'm not letting you leave when you're this tired. Besides, here you can rest and not have to answer questions about why you're in bed in the middle of the day."

She looked up at him. "I hate it when you have a point."

He smiled. "But at least you admit that I do have a point."

In answer, she shoved off her shoes and stretched out along the couch. He covered her with the blanket and, before he could stop himself, pushed a loose strand of hair away from her face. That gentle touch changed the air between them. When Savannah's eyes met his, he could tell that she sensed it, too.

"Sleep," he said simply, then forced himself to walk away before he crawled onto that couch with her.

But after she fell asleep, he couldn't stop himself from returning to the living room to simply look at her. He realized she was more relaxed than he'd seen her since they'd reconnected. A warmth filled him that he'd been able to give her that.

As he watched the gentle rise and fall of her chest, he realized he wanted to give her so much more.

Please, God, please let her be okay.

Chapter Ten

Savannah rolled onto her back and stretched, then reconsidered that motion. She grunted against twin jabs of pain, her bruised ribs on the left and the biopsy puncture on the right. Without opening her eyes, she took several deep breaths until the discomfort faded. Once it did, she realized that she felt more rested than she had in a while. Finally, she'd gotten a good night's sleep.

Her eyes popped open when she realized that what lay beneath her didn't feel like her bed. As she scanned her surroundings, everything came flooding back. Yep, definitely not her apartment. Her next thought was that she really had to go to the bathroom.

When she lifted herself from the couch, she didn't see Travis anywhere. She hurried down a hallway and found the bathroom. After tending to the most pressing matter, she looked at herself in the mirror and smoothed her hair. If she were home, she'd brush her teeth. But she had to settle for the next best thing and rinsed her mouth out with the mint mouthwash sitting atop the vanity. She splashed her face with cold water, which banished the final bit of grogginess.

She retraced her steps to the living room, arriving just as Travis came in through the front door.

"You're awake," he said.

"Yeah." She glanced at the clock on the wall and was stunned to see it was nearly 6:00 p.m. "You should have woke me hours ago."

"Why? You obviously needed the rest. How do you feel?"

"Sore." She paused as she met his gaze. "But rested."

His lips stretched into a satisfied smile.

She eyed the door behind him. "Did you go to work?"

"In a way. Went outside to make some calls so I wouldn't bother you."

"Travis, you shouldn't have let me run you from your house."

"You didn't. It's a nice day outside. Decided to soak up a few rays."

She laughed a little and shook her head.

Travis headed toward his kitchen. "Thirsty?"

She realized she was parched and followed him. "I'd kill for a glass of water."

"No killing necessary." He grabbed a glass from a cabinet and filled it with cold water from the tap.

"Thanks." She downed half the glass without stopping.

Travis grinned. "You were thirsty."

She'd probably been sleeping with her mouth wide-open. That surely made a pretty picture for him to see.

"So, any progress today?" The way he shifted his gaze away told her that she wasn't going to like the answer. "The lead didn't pan out, did it?"

"No."

"Tell me."

"Your mom was in Tulsa for a few weeks, staying with an aunt. But the aunt passed away a decade ago, and no one knows where your mother went from there."

Savannah set her glass down and leaned both hands

against the countertop. "How can someone just up and disappear, not once but twice?"

"It's easier than you might expect."

She shook her head. "Maybe it's not even worth trying. She obviously doesn't want to be found."

Travis closed the distance between them and turned her to face him. He lifted her chin so that she met his gaze.

"Don't give up hope yet. I'm not done looking, not by a long shot." He ran his thumb over her bottom lip.

In the blink of an eye, the moment changed from him reassuring her to something very different. His expression changed to what she'd swear was hunger right before he dropped his lips to hers.

She felt that restrained hunger as his mouth took possession of hers, and she silently cursed her injuries. Because right now she wanted nothing more than to be healthy and whole and to satisfy her own hunger for this man.

Gradually, Travis pulled away but leaned his forehead against hers. "I'm sorry."

"Don't be. I quite liked it."

He smiled and kissed her again, soft and sweet this time. "No, I'm sorry to start something I can't finish."

Her heart gave an extra hard thump against her chest. At least part of Travis wanted what she wanted, and that knowledge sent a zing of excitement through her. But there was obvious struggling with his new and probably unexpected desire. "I should go."

This time, he didn't disagree.

She lifted onto her toes and gave him one last kiss before forcing herself out the front door. Despite everything—the fruitless lead in the search for her mother, her still uncertain health status, the yearning for Travis that went unfulfilled—she still wore a smile all the way home.

EVEN THOUGH HIS self-protective instincts told Travis to stay away from Savannah, he couldn't. Over the next several days, he drove out to the ranch at least once a day. He had nothing new to report on the search for her mother, but thankfully she didn't seem to mind that he showed up empty-handed. Well, not exactly empty-handed. He'd brought her flowers one day, takeout from Amos's another and plenty of kisses every time.

In fact, it was getting harder and harder to give her the necessary time to heal, harder to resist the need in him that had been neglected for too long. Thoughts of her didn't even let him be while he was sleeping, and his dreams only made him hungry for her even more.

When he wasn't with her, he devoted most of his time to the search for Delia, going down every path he could think of to take. They all turned up nothing, at least until an email from a colleague in Galveston landed in his inbox. He sped through it then read it more carefully before printing it out and shoving it into his pocket. He grabbed his keys and headed for the door.

"By the speed at which you're moving, I'm guessing you're going to see Savannah." Blossom said Savannah's name in a teasing, singsong voice.

"As a matter of fact I am." He saluted Blossom and headed out to the elevator.

"Have enough fun for me!"

He smiled because he planned to. Maybe not tonight, but eventually he wanted to pull Savannah into his arms and not let her go until they both were satisfied.

When he reached the Peach Pit, he was glad to see that Savannah's vehicle was the only one in the lot. Needing to be near her, he strode inside, all the way back to the kitchen, and pulled her into his arms. She squealed in surprise but melted against him when he captured her mouth.

The kiss went from zero to sixty in a fraction of a second, with Savannah's hands snaking their way through his hair. But as if she suddenly corralled some common sense, she pulled away, trying to catch her breath.

"What was that for?"

He grinned. "Do I need a reason?"

For a moment she looked flustered and glanced beyond him as if to make sure no one was around. It was cute.

"I want you to come away with me this weekend, to Galveston."

"What?"

"I got another lead, a solid one this time."

Savannah held up a hand. "Travis, don't…"

He'd given himself permission to live again, to maybe even love again, no matter how scary that prospect. He wasn't letting her shut down this idea before he got it out, convinced her it was just what they needed in more ways than one.

"I rented us a beach cottage, so we can have a nice getaway while also seeing if this new information leads us to your mom."

Savannah's eyes widened as she glanced beyond him again.

He looked over his shoulder and immediately realized his mistake. His assumption that Savannah was alone had been wrong. Carly stood in the doorway to the storeroom, a stack of aluminum pie pans in her hands and a stunned expression on her normally peppy face.

"What's he talking about, Savannah?"

Savannah took a step toward her sister. "Carly, it's nothing."

Carly held up a hand. "No. I distinctly heard him mention Mom. Are you looking for her?"

Savannah shot him a desperate look, as if he might be

able to reverse the last couple of minutes like a DVR recording. He hoped she saw the apology in his eyes. She took a deep breath, resigned, and shifted her attention back to Carly.

"Yes, I'm looking for Mom, and Travis is helping me."

"And you didn't think you should tell me? Does anyone else know?"

"No, just Travis."

"I don't understand. Didn't you think maybe you're not the only one who has questions to ask her?"

He heard the hurt in Carly's voice, the same kind he knew was a part of Savannah.

"It was a sudden decision. I… One of the things I wanted to know was our family medical history on Mom's side."

"This because of Lizzie and the baby?"

Savannah hesitated before answering. "No, this is for me."

Carly's forehead furrowed. "Why? You two planning to have a kid or something?"

"No!"

He didn't know why, but Savannah's quick, forceful answer kicked him in the gut. He'd never given much thought to having kids, especially after Corinne's death. But now? With Savannah? He was surprised to find he didn't mind the idea.

Savannah took a couple of steps toward the middle of the room and leaned back against a table that stood in the center of the kitchen, one on which she'd rolled out pie dough. "After I got hurt at the rodeo, I found a lump in my breast. The doctor asked if there was a history of breast cancer in the family, and I realized I didn't know the answer. I have no idea about a lot of things regarding Mom, like why she up and left us."

"You found a lump? What did the doctor say?"

Savannah gripped the edge of the table, and Travis wanted so much to pull her into his arms. But this was between her and Carly. Truthfully, he should leave, but he suspected it would be more awkward for her were he to walk away in the middle of all this than to stand silently on the sidelines, waiting to give Savannah support if she needed it. He fought the old need to distance himself from potential loss. He wondered if he'd ever truly conquer it or if it would always be there, whispering to him to shield his heart, to keep others at arm's length.

"I had a biopsy on Monday." Savannah glanced his way and gave him a little smile. "Travis was kind enough to go with me."

"You took a stranger instead of your sister?"

"Carly," Savannah said, sounding for a moment like the scolding older sister. "Travis isn't a stranger."

Carly shot him a look filled with anger, but as he watched he saw it drain away.

"I know. Sorry."

"It's okay," he said.

Savannah pushed away from the table and faced her sister. "I didn't want to worry you or anyone else in the family. And I didn't want to have to answer a million questions. You know how I am. I prefer to deal with things on my own."

"But you're okay, right?"

Savannah pressed her lips together for a moment. "I don't know yet. I'm still waiting for the biopsy results."

"You're okay." Carly sounded as if she knew for certain, or at least was trying to will Savannah's good health into existence. Travis understood the need to do that.

"I hope you're right."

"Of course I am." Carly crossed to her sister and took

Savannah's hands in hers. "And I'm glad you're looking for Mom. I want those answers, too."

"I need you to not tell anyone else. I don't want to have to deal with that right now."

"Don't worry. I know Dad would crap a brick."

Carly's accurate assessment of their father's reaction sat there in the air for a moment before Savannah snorted. In the next beat, they were all laughing. It was just what they all needed.

SAVANNAH HAD THOUGHT she was doing the right thing by keeping her health condition and the search for her mother secret, but she felt loads lighter after she spent a couple of hours telling Carly everything.

"Is there anything I can do to help? I mean, I remember even less about Mom than you do, but I feel as if I should do something."

"Beyond keeping it under wraps for now, no. I'm really relying on Travis at this point."

"Yeah, about Travis. I also heard that part about him asking you to go away for the weekend."

Savannah hadn't had time to process that tidbit before Carly had walked in on the conversation. A weekend at the beach, alone with Travis? That sounded wonderful.

"I could deal with another hot brother-in-law."

Savannah laughed. "Getting a little ahead of yourself, aren't you?"

"Not really. I've never seen you look at someone the way you do him. And you get all jittery and flushed when he shows up."

"Because I always wonder if he's found Mom yet."

"Oh, please. I'm not a little kid you can fib to anymore. You have the hots for him just as much as he does you. I'd even place good money on the fact that you're falling for him."

Savannah didn't confirm or deny, but she knew her sister was right. Every day, a little more of her heart became his.

"I'm right, aren't I?"

"Maybe."

"Then you should go to the beach with him. Even if the lead on Mom doesn't amount to anything, it's still a beach weekend with a hot guy. Not that I think you'll be leaving the cottage much."

"Carly!"

"What? Tell me you haven't thought about it? Wait, have you done it yet? Because he looks like he'd be good in bed."

Savannah's face flushed what had to be tomato-red, which of course only egged Carly on.

"Look at you!"

"You're being a twit."

"So, have you or haven't you?"

Savannah sighed. "No, we haven't."

Carly shot up from where she'd been sitting crosslegged in the comfy living-room chair. "Well, then, we need to get you packed."

"I can't just up and run off for the weekend. I have a business to run, one that Dad is half convinced is going to fail anyway. I don't need to add fuel to that fire."

Carly waved away her concern. "Don't worry about the store. I think Gina and I can handle it."

"And what if someone asks where I've gone?"

"Easy. I tell them you've gone away with a friend for the weekend." Carly started walking toward the bedroom, ticking off a list of everything Savannah needed to pack. "A razor, some nice-smelling lotion, a sexy nightie."

"I don't even own a sexy nightie. The sexiest sleep-wear I have is an old T-shirt that's so worn that it's nearly see-through."

Carly rolled her eyes. "Well, grab your purse then."

"Why?"

"Because I'm taking you shopping."

The next thing Savannah knew, Carly had dragged her out to her car and they were headed to a lingerie store in Dallas.

"Text loverboy and tell him to pick you up bright and early in the morning."

Savannah started to object, feeling the need to regain some control of her suddenly runaway life.

"Do it or I'll pull this car over and do it myself. You and that eye candy are going to the beach, and when you come back you're going to tell me all about it in minute detail."

Her fingers shaking, Savannah texted Travis. She'd barely taken a breath before the return text hit her phone.

See you then was followed by a smiley face.

By this time tomorrow, she was going to be alone with Travis where no one could interrupt them. She turned her face toward the passenger window so her sister couldn't see the wide smile that she could no longer keep hidden.

Chapter Eleven

Savannah watched as Travis effortlessly carried her luggage up the wooden steps to their beach cottage. She was halfway afraid that he could see through the suitcase to the sexy blue nightie Carly had forced her to buy the night before, not to mention the three new sets of underwear.

She took a deep breath of salty sea air and hoped she could relax and enjoy herself. She'd hoped to have news one way or the other on the biopsy by now, but she was still waiting. Still didn't know whether cancer was growing inside her at that very moment. Was it fair to Travis, or to herself, to allow their relationship to take the next step until she knew her prognosis?

She'd posed the same question to Carly. In a moment of more maturity and seriousness than her sister usually displayed, she'd said, "Travis is a grown man. Let him make his own decision."

If the way he'd looked at her and held her hand all the way to the beach was any indication, his decision had been made. And yet, she still sensed a wariness in him that he might not even be consciously aware of himself.

"You coming in?" he called down from the landing.

She did her best to shove away her worries and smiled up at him. "Yeah. Be right there."

The cottage was adorable, and for a moment she wondered what it would be like to live somewhere like this all the time. She loved the ranch, but there was something about the ocean that was so relaxing. It was as if the waves were there solely for the purpose of washing your cares out to sea.

"Are you hungry?" Travis asked as he came up behind where she was staring out the glass balcony doors.

"Starving."

"Good. There's a little place right on the beach not far from here."

They ate at a quaint, open-air restaurant then took a short walk on the beach before her anxiety got the better of her and stopped her in her tracks.

Travis turned toward her. "You okay?"

"I'm sorry. I don't think I'm going to be very good company until we follow up on this lead you have."

If she had to wait on her test results, she didn't want to wait to take the next step in the search for her mother.

He looked as if he wanted to put it off for a while longer, and she understood why. They were having a nice time, and that might change if this lead on her mother's whereabouts proved as useless as the first one.

But Travis had seemed excited by it, had said that it was a more solid lead. She was hanging on to that knowledge with both hands and had to see this through. She had to have an answer to at least one of the questions hanging over her head.

"Okay," he said as he took her hand and turned them back toward the restaurant parking lot.

It didn't take long to get from the Crab Hut to a short street off the beaten path lined with small, pastel-colored mobile homes. The whole street had a retro fifties vibe. Travis pulled up in front of one of the trailers that had a faded pink exterior. The sandy yard was filled with flowcrpots overflowing with colorful bougainvillea and at least half a dozen other types of flowers.

"So this is where she lived?"

"Somewhere on the other side of the street," Travis said.

On the drive that morning, he'd told her everything he'd learned so far. About a year after her mother left Oklahoma, she'd settled here. The only person who still lived on Conch Lane from that time was Phyllis O'Donnell, evidently the resident of the pink trailer.

Savannah placed her hand on her swirling stomach.

Travis clasped her other hand and squeezed. "You ready?"

She nodded once. "Ready as I'm ever going to be."

She allowed Travis to lead the way up the flagstone path to the front door. He only had to knock once before an elderly lady with pink curlers in her hair answered.

"Yes?"

"Mrs. O'Donnell, my name is Travis Shepard. You talked to a colleague of mine, Matt Ferguson."

"Oh, yes. You wanted to know about Dee."

The name threw Savannah for a moment until she realized that if her mother had wanted to stay hidden, she might have changed the name she went by. And Dee was simply a shortened version of Delia and thus easy to remember.

Mrs. O'Donnell opened the door. "Come on in." She shifted her hand to her hair. "Sorry about the curlers. I've been running a bit behind this morning. Got behind one of those super couponers at the store. Took her half an hour to check out."

"It's okay," Savannah said. "A gal's got to do what a gal's got to do."

"Ain't that right?" Mrs. O'Donnell giggled and waved

thcm into the living area. A plate of cookies sat on the coffee table. "I just made those lemon cookies this morning. Now can I offer you both a cup of coffee? Water or soda maybe?"

Both Savannah and Travis acccptcd a cup of coffee, and Savannah grabbed a cookie just to have something to do with her free hand. But when she took a bite, she was surprised by how good it was.

"This is delicious."

Mrs. O'Donnell smiled. "Why, thank you, dear. I've been making those for probably fifty years. Was my mama's recipe. I'll give it to you if you like."

"That would be great. Thank you."

"Speaking of mothers," Travis said, shifting the conversation. "The reason we wanted to know about your neighbor Dee is that we believe she's the same woman who went by the name Delia Baron, Savannah's mother."

Mrs. O'Donnell turned her gaze toward Savannah. "You know, I can see the resemblance now."

Excitement sparked to life inside Savannah, replacing the anxiety. "What do you remember about her?"

"Well, now. I've been thinking on that since I talked to your friend, Matt. Nice boy, that Matt." Mrs. O'Donnell scratched a spot on her head between two of the rollers. "I guess it's been between fifteen and twenty years ago. I'm sorry, but I can't remember exactly. My memory isn't what it once was. But I remember Dee was a sweet thing, but sad. I just wanted to give her a hug and tell her life was full of beautiful things to enjoy. Even though she was always kind to all her neighbors, I don't think the sadness ever went away."

Savannah had the uncharitable thought that it wasn't a surprise that abandoning one's family might make one a little sad.

"I only saw sadness like that one other time, after my sister lost a baby. Even though she went on about her life, she never got over that loss."

Savannah glanced at Travis, who looked in her direction at the same time before shifting his attention back to Mrs. O'Donnell.

Could her mother have experienced the same thing even though she hadn't lost a baby but had instead walked away from her children? Then why walk away? Why not come back?

"Did she ever talk about her family?" Travis asked.

The elderly woman shook her head. "No, I got the sense she was alone in the world. I never saw anyone come over to her place other than those of us who lived on this street. We'd switch up going to each other's places to play cards or board games. Oh, I remember Dee made the absolute best peach pie you've ever put in your mouth."

Savannah sucked in a breath.

Travis reached over and took her hand, giving her a much-needed anchor.

"Do you know where she is now?" Savannah knew she sounded desperate, but this was the closest she'd been to her mother since the day she'd disappeared from her life. Her heart sank as she saw Mrs. O'Donnell shake her head.

"I'm sorry, dear. Dee lived across the street, in the little mint-green trailer, for maybe three years. Then one day she moved away in the middle of the night without telling anyone. But she left all of us a peach pie on our porches. I thought that was so nice, but I wondered about her for a long time."

"You never heard from her again?" Travis asked.

"No. I don't even know where she went. We often wondered afterward if she was hiding from someone, and the someone got too close."

Savannah wondered if her father had looked for her mom. That didn't seem likely considering he wouldn't even speak Delia's name now, pretended as if she'd never existed.

Though her heart sat heavy in her chest, Savannah nevertheless soaked up the stories about her mother that Mrs. O'Donnell shared. Tales of rowdy ladies' poker games, helping each other evacuate ahead of a hurricane, of donations of baked goods to every local charity imaginable.

When Mrs. O'Donnell had finally exhausted what she could remember, Savannah leaned forward and took the older woman's wrinkled hands in hers. "Thank you for sharing your memories with me. They mean a lot."

"I'm sorry I couldn't help you more. You seem like a sweet girl."

As Travis drove them back toward the beach cottage a few minutes later, Savannah fought against the encroaching sense of sadness and despair. While she'd discovered information about a slice of her mother's life, she also had come away with more questions. Why had her mother picked Galveston as a temporary home? Why had she been so sad, especially when she could have done something about it? And why did she leave here as suddenly as she had her home at the ranch?

Travis seemed to understand she needed quiet. He simply held her hand as he drove. When they reached the cottage and walked inside, he finally pulled her into his arms.

"We'll find her. We're closer than we were this morning."

"Are we?"

"I'm not going to tell you that you'll get your answers quickly, but you'll get them. We'll find your mother."

She smiled at him, at least as much as she could manage at the moment. "I'm really tired. I think I'll go take a nap."

She saw the worry in his eyes, but he didn't force her to talk more. He simply dropped a light kiss on her forehead and stepped away. For a moment, she wanted to pull him back to her, to take him to bed, but that wouldn't be fair to him. She didn't want to use him to feel good in the face of heartbreaking news.

Despite a fatigue that she suspected had more to do with the weight on her heart than the limited sleep she'd gotten the night before, she couldn't fall asleep. After tossing and turning for more than an hour, she got up and slipped out the door from the bedroom to the balcony. The soothing sound of the waves beckoned, so she headed for the beach. Part of her knew she should tell Travis where she was going, but she just wanted to be alone with her thoughts.

She walked slowly through the edge of the surf on the packed sand, letting the salty water roll softly over her feet. All the details Mrs. O'Donnell had shared about Delia replayed in Savannah's mind. The thought of her mom making peach pies for her neighbors actually helped her smile.

She remembered the day about a year after her mother had left that she found her mom's peach pie recipe in the kitchen. She'd baked it for her dad, thinking it would make him happy. It'd had the opposite effect, and Savannah had hidden the recipe away in her room for fear her dad would destroy the note card on which her mother had written it. At that time, she'd still held out hope that her mother would return, if Savannah just held on tightly enough, wished hard enough. Even though all her wishing hadn't worked, she still had that card, used the recipe every day to make the pies she sold in the Peach Pit.

Her gaze lit on a snowy-white seashell half buried in the sand, and she leaned over to pick it up. It turned out to be an intact angel wing. She ran her fingertips along the delicate ridges and felt the oddest sensation that it was a sign. A sign of what, she had no idea.

She rinsed the sand off the shell with the next incoming wave, then walked farther up the beach to a dry spot and sat down. As she stared out at the horizon, she wondered if she should continue her search. Was she to take today's revelations as the impetus to keep looking or a warning that every lead was going to end in heartbreak?

A tear escaped and ran down her cheek just as she realized someone was approaching. She swiped the tear away and turned to see Travis.

"Mind if I join you, or do you want to be alone?"

She patted the sand beside her. Being alone hadn't provided any concrete answers to the questions swirling in her head. At least with Travis here, she'd have the comfort of his presence.

He sat and propped his arms on his knees as he stared out at the Gulf of Mexico. "Makes you wonder why any of us live inland, doesn't it?"

She smiled a little. "I'm guessing it would lose its appeal if everyone lived here. Or when a hurricane was bearing down."

"There is that."

She realized as she sat there looking out at a landscape so different from the one she was used to seeing that she wouldn't have her life any other way. Maybe she didn't get to smell sea air every day, but the ranch was a part of her. She'd sunk not only her hard work and creativity into the Peach Pit but also her heart. Maybe finding her mother wasn't what was important. She had brothers and sisters, a father and stepmother, people who were important parts of her life. And she'd soon be an aunt and would have another youngster besides Julieta's son, Alex, to spoil with treats and gifts.

Maybe that should be enough. She felt the need to draw inward, to cocoon.

"Thank you for trying to find my mom."

Travis looked at her. "You're not giving up, are you?"

"I just don't know if I'm strong enough to go through this over and over."

"You don't have to. I don't have to update you all the time, getting you invested in leads that might not pan out. I can keep looking and not tell you anything unless I do find her."

She hugged her knees close to her chest. "I'm not sure that would be any better. I'd always be wondering. Maybe it's best if I just cut ties once and for all."

Travis cupped her jaw, running his thumb across her cheek. "I hope you don't mean ties to me."

"Travis—"

"Because I'm not letting you."

In the next moment, his lips captured hers in a kiss that sent zings of sexual awareness shooting to all her extremities. Travis pulled her close, and her hunger for him increased until she was ravenous. She might not have her mother, or even answers about her own future, but at the moment she had a wonderful, sexy man in her arms.

"Come back to the cottage with me," he whispered against her lips.

"Okay."

As if he thought she might change her mind, Travis jumped to his feet and extended his hand to her. She placed hers in his and laughed when he pulled her up so quickly that she stumbled against him.

"Don't know your own strength?"

His smile was wicked. "I knew exactly what I was doing."

And then he kissed her again, so deeply that she had to grip his shoulders to stay on her feet. As he took her hand and led her back toward the cottage, it was all she could do not to ask him to run. Because she was done putting off what she wanted. Everything else in her life might be full of questions but not the fact that she wanted to make love to Travis.

They nearly tripped over their own feet as they hurried up the wooden steps to the cottage. As soon as they stepped through the bedroom door, Travis spun her into his arms again. His kiss stoked the fire already building inside her.

"I can't seem to get enough of you," he said.

"The feeling's mutual."

"So what are we going to do about it?"

She met his teasing by running her hands underneath the T-shirt he wore. "I don't know about you, but I'm going to satisfy my curiosity."

"About?"

"What these muscles feel like. I've been wondering that since the morning I walked into my living room to see you stretched out on my couch shirtless."

He lifted a brow. "You could have satisfied your curiosity then."

"I wasn't ready then." She didn't think he had been, either.

"And you are now."

It wasn't a question, but she answered anyway by shoving his shirt up and over his head. The sight of all that masculine skin, the feel of the cut muscles underneath her fingertips nearly made her pant like an animal.

Travis eased his warm hands underneath her shirt,

skimming her stomach. "Seems unfair for me to be shirtless and you still covered."

She met his eyes. "You're right. What are you going to do about it?"

A hint of a smile played at the edges of his mouth as his hands slid slowly upward over her stomach until they rested on her breasts. His fingers teased at the edge of her bra, one of the new ones she'd bought the night before. At the moment, she couldn't remember what color it was and didn't care.

With agonizingly slow movements, Travis lifted her shirt over her head and tossed it across a lounge chair in the corner. He captured her lips again for a dizzying kiss before letting his mouth trail along her neck and then down to the swell of breast above her bra. In the next moment, he'd unclasped her bra and guided it down her arms. That warm, wet, talented mouth of his captured her left breast, causing a moan of pleasure to escape her.

He kissed, licked and suckled her until she was in danger of collapsing.

"I want to make love to you, Savannah, so bad."

"I want that, too. Now."

She gasped when he scooped her up into his arms as if she weighed next to nothing and carried her to the bed. He paused to rub his fingers gingerly over the fading bruising on her ribs.

"Am I going to hurt you?"

Such a simple question, but it carried an incredible impact, so much caring. Savannah lifted her hand to his face and cupped his strong jaw. "No."

Despite her answer, he was careful as he lay down beside her and pulled her close, capturing her mouth once again. Within moments, however, he seemed to forget his resolve to be gentle. The kiss grew more heated, yearning, desperate. The feel of her naked breasts against the warm skin of his chest made her body throb for even more contact.

"Make love to me, Travis."

Within moments, he'd divested her of her shorts and underwear and quickly stood to remove his jeans and boxers and sheath himself. Savannah's mouth watered when he stood before her naked, the setting sun providing an orange glow behind him.

He joined her in the bed again, and words were put aside, replaced by caresses, kisses, a tangle of legs and the need to be even closer. Travis's hand skimmed the curve of her hip before he moved it between her legs at the same time he used his thigh to nudge her legs apart. He teased her sensitive flesh, and she groaned into his mouth. His ministrations seemed to go on forever, driving her crazy with wanting, before he slipped a finger inside her.

Instinctively, she pressed harder against him. Travis rolled her onto her back, and her heart sped up at the wonderful weight of him.

His mouth moved to her ear, nibbling, then nuzzled her neck as his finger continued to circle and probe. He continued trailing his mouth down her neck until he captured her right breast this time. Her thoughts flew to the lump inside, but when Travis's tongue darted against the tip she could think of nothing else but the pressure building in her middle, the absolute ecstasy of having her body tasted by this man.

"Travis," she breathed as she ran her hands through his hair, pressing him closer.

As if he understood that the sound of his name on her lips was a plea, he removed his hand from within her. He captured her whimper with his mouth on hers as he slipped the length of him inside her. Without thinking, she rose up to meet him.

"Damn, you feel good," he said, his breath ragged.

She ran her hands down his back until they reached his hips and dug into that firm flesh.

There was no more waiting, no more being slow and careful. Travis pulled almost all the way out before thrusting into her again. She cried out as she threw her head back against the pillow.

Travis lifted his head. "Did I hurt you?"

"No," she gasped. "And stop talking."

The smile of male satisfaction that spread across his face made her dig her fingers deeper into his flesh. He reacted by pressing farther into her, then kissing her with so much passion that she instinctively spread her legs wider.

Travis ran his fingers up the inner part of her thighs before sliding his palms beneath her hips. The next thrust came faster, the one that followed faster still. As his pace increased, so did Savannah's breathing until she was gasping for breath. She loved the feel of his firm hips beneath her hands, the way they tightened with each thrust. The faster he moved, the closer she felt herself getting to release.

"Keep going, don't stop," she said next to his ear.

He complied, seeming to do the impossible by driving into her even faster.

There, there, she…was…almost…

Savannah gave the intensity of her release a voice by crying out Travis's name. She was still riding the wave when she felt him tense all over. As she managed to focus on him above her, he threw back his head and thrust one more time before finding his own release. She'd swear he growled like an animal, and the muscles were stretched taut in his arms and neck. Unable to keep from touching him, she ran her hand down his sweat-slicked chest.

When Travis met her eyes, she saw an intensity in his that made the deepest part of her sing. She knew without a doubt that she was totally in love with him.

Chapter Twelve

Travis fell back onto the bed, totally wiped out. But he'd swear at the moment that he'd never felt better in his life. A twinge of guilt tugged at him as he forcefully shifted his thoughts to intimate times with Corinne. There wasn't an ounce of doubt in his mind that he'd loved her, that he'd enjoyed making love to her, but this? Now with Savannah? Perhaps the all-consuming happiness he felt at the moment was just the product of how recently he'd had sex, but he didn't think so.

Savannah ran her fingertips down the middle of his chest. "What are you thinking?"

He would not tell her he'd been thinking of his wife. Instead, he turned his head toward her. "That I'm not sure if I'm ever going to be able to walk again."

Her cheeks pinkened as she smiled, and he couldn't resist touching her. He pulled her next to him, and she laid her head on his shoulder. This, right now, was life at its best.

"I've never done that before," she said.

"Had sex?" he teased.

She playfully swatted his arm. "I've had sex." She gestured toward the windows. "Just not with the blinds wide-open where anyone could see."

"They can't see us from the beach. And even if they could, I guess we gave them a good show."

She made a sound of shocked surprise and poked him in the side.

He laughed and kissed her on the forehead. "It was wonderful, Savannah." He paused before he went on, wondering if he should say what he was thinking. But what they'd just shared had only convinced him further that he was falling in love with her, no matter how he'd once thought that impossible. "It's the first time since Corinne."

Savannah pulled back to look at him. "Really?"

He nodded. "Just didn't seem right."

"And now?"

He heard the concern in her voice and wanted to reassure her. "Nothing has ever seemed more right."

They kissed for a while, and he was beginning to be ready to go again when he realized that Savannah was tired. So instead of sating his building need for her, he allowed her to snuggle next to him and fall asleep. Carefully, he pulled the sheet up to cover their bodies. But when he caught sight of her naked breast, he stopped. He'd give anything to know for sure that she was perfectly healthy. While they'd made love, he'd been able to forget the fact that she might have cancer, that she could be ripped from him too soon as Corinne had been.

He didn't want to think that way, but it was impossible not to. When you'd been through an unexpected loss, you began to expect the same thing everywhere you turned. The fact that he hadn't had sex with anyone else since Corinne's passing was probably just him protecting himself. But he hadn't done so with Savannah, and that self-protective instinct wondered if he'd made a mistake. Was it already too late to pull away, even if he thought he'd have the strength to do so?

Though he wanted to be strong and positive for her, he felt too weak to keep the negative thoughts out of his head. They followed him into slumber and plagued his dreams, causing him to wake with a start sometime later.

"You okay?"

Her voice came from across the dark room. When he looked that direction, he saw her outline next to the window.

"Yeah, fine. What are you doing?"

"I'm too embarrassed to say."

"Oh, yeah?" He shifted off the bed and walked toward her. "This I've got to hear."

"No."

He lifted her chin. "What?"

"I was just wondering…"

"Wondering?"

"What it's like to make love out on the beach, under the stars."

Travis went instantly hard at the thought. He pulled her close and placed his lips next to her ear. "I say we find out."

A couple of minutes later, they hurried down the steps to the sand below.

Savannah held his hand with one of hers and grasped a couple of blankets under her other arm. "I can't believe we're doing this. What if someone sees us?"

"It's the middle of the night. Most people are asleep."

"We're not. Maybe some people like to go for walks on the beach at this hour."

At the bottom of the steps, he turned toward her and dropped a kiss on her sweet lips. "That's what the blankets are for."

Travis felt like laughing as they hurried down to the beach. He remembered seeing an area a short distance from the cottage, a sort of natural alcove hidden by the dunes. He led Savannah there and spread one of the blankets. They lay down side by side facing the clear, starfilled sky.

"It's beautiful," she said.

He shifted to his side to look at her. "So are you. I've always thought so."

She laughed a little, as if she didn't believe him.

"It's true. I had a crush on you in high school."

She met his gaze, and even in the dim light he could see the disbelief.

"No, you didn't."

"I assure you, I did. I tried so many times to tell you, but I bungled it every time. Besides, your one true love was barrel racing back then."

"But Corinne?"

Travis pushed Savannah's hair behind her ear. "I moved on, fell in love, got married."

"I never told you how sorry I was about Corinne. She was a lovely person."

"Yeah, she was. I felt guilty about her death for a long time. Still do sometimes."

Savannah caressed his cheek. "It wasn't your fault."

"It was my fault that I wasn't here. I was thousands of miles away."

"Even if you had been here, it likely wouldn't have changed anything."

His heart ached with old pain. "I'll never know for sure. She might not have stopped at that gas station that day. We could have been on vacation, at home, out to eat, anywhere but there."

"You are no more at fault for Corinne's death than I am for my mother leaving."

"It's not the same. Your mother is still out there some-where."

"We don't know that, either. What I do know is that I wondered if I'd done something to make my mom run away. That's what happens when you're a little kid and your mother leaves a note on the kitchen table saying she can't stay anymore, that she needs to be alone."

Travis pulled Savannah close. "It wasn't anything you did."

"I know that now. And you have to believe that what happened to Corinne was no one's fault but that man who shot her."

Somewhere down deep, he knew that. But that didn't make it any easier to totally absolve himself. Corinne had died alone, and he had to live with that. As he looked into Savannah's eyes, however, he realized he wanted to move on. "You're amazing, always have been."

"Not really. I'm just a girl who likes horses and bak-ing pies."

He placed his palm against her chest. "And who has a kind heart."

Travis pulled the second blanket over the top of them and kissed Savannah. Slowly, they made their way out of their clothes and made love under the wide Texas sky. As he opened his heart up to her, he felt the old wall he'd built around it beginning to crumble and fall away.

SAVANNAH HAD NEVER had a better weekend, not even when she was at the height of her winning years on the rodeo circuit. Considering her health was still uncertain and she felt no closer to finding her mother and the answers she realized were still important, her happiness was even more amazing. But she'd never felt closer to anyone in her life than she did Travis. That didn't seem reasonable, possible, but it was no less true.

They took long walks on the beach, talking about everything that had happened to each of them in the years since high school. He took her to eat fresh seafood, scrumptious pizza and French pastries at a tiny bakery called Délicieux. They sat on the deck holding hands and watched the gorgeous sunrise. And they spent a good bit of time in bed, discovering all the curves and pleasures of each other's bodies.

She watched him sleep now, letting herself wonder what it would be like if the weekend didn't have to end, if she could wake up every morning and see his handsome face, feel his reassuring warmth.

"Why are you staring at me?" Travis asked without opening his eyes.

"How did you know that?"

He opened one eye. "Because I'm just that good."

She elbowed him in the ribs, which led to him trying to tickle hers. "Stop it!"

"Never." He laughed and rolled atop her and started tickling her unmercifully.

"Uncle, uncle!"

Travis dropped his lips to just above hers. "That's not what I want to hear you say."

She nipped at his bottom lip with her teeth. "What do you want to hear?"

"Just what you want me to do."

"Fix me breakfast?"

He lifted a brow. "Eventually. But first things first."

They made love again, slowly, sensuously, as if it were the last time. Fear shot through her at that thought.

Please don't let this be the last time. She pleaded with God, the universe, fate—whomever or whatever was in control. *Please don't take this away when I've just found out what love really feels like.*

When they lay nestled against each other afterward, she drew lazy circles on his chest with her finger. "I don't want to go back to the real world."

"Me, neither."

"Can't we stay here forever?"

"I would like nothing more."

She sighed, knowing it was a fantasy.

Travis made good on feeding her breakfast, though he didn't cook it. When they left the restaurant where she'd indulged in a big stack of buttermilk pancakes with warm maple syrup, she pulled Travis to a stop halfway back to the car.

"Thank you for bringing me here."

"To Mama's Country Cooking?"

She smiled, even loving the way he teased her. "No, to Galveston."

He pulled her into the circle of his arms. "Even though we struck out on the search again?"

"That wasn't the most important part of this weekend, at least not for me. I've loved every minute with you."

"The feeling's mutual." He kissed her right there in the parking lot, and she realized that no matter where she was it would always be romantic with him.

"I've got one more thing I'd like to do before we leave."

"I'm not sure I have any stamina left, woman, but I'll do my best."

A part of her wanted to take him up on the offer, but if they went back to bed they'd never make the checkout time. "Unless you want some poor cleaning lady to walk in on us, I think you should just take me to the grocery."

As they headed away from the cottage two hours and one quick lovemaking session later, Travis drove the short distance to Mrs. O'Donnell's trailer.

"I'll just be a minute," Savannah said as she hopped out, the warm peach pie in hand.

When Mrs. O'Donnell opened the door, her eyes brightened. "I didn't expect to see you again, dear."

Savannah lifted the pie. "I thought you might like this."

"You didn't have to bring me anything."

"It's peach. I think you'll recognize the recipe."

Savannah's heart squeezed when Mrs. O'Donnell accepted the pie, and tears welled in her eyes. And no matter why her mother had left, Savannah was glad she'd had this woman as a friend.

"Won't you come in and have a piece?" She looked toward the SUV. "And bring that nice boy with you, too."

"I'm sorry, but we're on our way home."

The older woman nodded in understanding. "Just a minute, then. I found something I think you should have."

Savannah couldn't imagine what it might be, but she didn't have to wait long to find out. Mrs. O'Donnell extended a photo to her. Hand shaking, Savannah took it and looked at the image. Her mother's face stared back at her as she stood with four other women. Mrs. O'Donnell had been right. Despite the smile on her mother's face, there was a profound sadness in her eyes. Savannah bit her bottom lip to keep from crying.

"Thank you for letting me see this, but I can't take your photo."

"Sure you can. I got a copy made down at the pharmacy."

Touched by Mrs. O'Donnell's generosity, Savannah hugged the woman before hurrying back to the vehicle.

"You okay?" Travis asked when she slipped into her seat.

"Yeah." She showed him the picture. "We might not have found my mom, but this at least proves she was here."

Travis took her hand and brought it to his lips. "Baby steps."

She nodded then looked out the window to wave at Mrs. O'Donnell as Travis headed them toward home.

When they arrived back at her apartment, Savannah prepared for some teasing from Carly, especially since Travis carried in her luggage. But the look on her sister's face halted Savannah.

"What's wrong?"

"Dad wants to see you."

Savannah sighed. "I'm tired. I'll go see him tomorrow."

"No, he was very explicit. He said for you to come to the house the moment you got back from wherever you'd 'traipsed off to.'" Carly fidgeted with the order pad on the counter, and Carly wasn't a fidgeter.

"What? You didn't tell him anything, did you?"

Carly shook her head. "No. Your secret is safe. But, he made me bring him the latest financials for the store. He looked like a man on a mission, and I don't think it's one you're going to like."

Savannah's heart sank to the floor. Would her father really close the store against her wishes? Why would he push her away like that? A rush of determination propelled her toward the door. Fine. If he wanted to have this conversation, they were having it. But she wasn't about to be a meek little daughter acquiescing to his every wish. She wasn't giving up without a fight.

Travis, proving he was a wise man, didn't say much but also didn't let her get behind the wheel of her car, either. In her current agitated state, she'd probably mow someone down without realizing it. When they reached the house where she'd grown up, she started to storm inside until Travis caught her by the arm.

"You don't want to face him like this," he said.

"Yeah, I do."

"It's been a while since I've seen your dad, but I don't think attacking him is the best way to win the day."

Savannah growled in frustration. "Why do you have to be smart *and* sexy?"

He shot her a crooked grin. "Sexy, huh?"

"Not that you need ego stroking, but yeah. I didn't exactly spend the weekend in bed with you because you're butt ugly, you know."

Heedless of who might be watching, Travis pulled her to him and kissed her as if he meant it. The feel of him, firm and solid and still tasting like the vanilla cone he'd had on the trip back, made her want to drag him off to the nearest bed. But first she had to deal with her father.

With a slightly cooler head, she headed into the house. Her dad might wonder at Travis's presence at her side, but she wasn't about to push away the man she loved. Her resolve faltered momentarily as she stepped into her dad's office to find him sitting on the couch with his broken leg propped on the ottoman, papers and file folders scattered around him.

"So you've finally returned, I see," her dad said even before he looked at her. He'd always done that, and she'd always found it unnerving. She wondered if he used the same tactic in his business dealings, disarming others in order to get what he wanted.

When he finally did look toward her, his eyes narrowed on Travis. Her heart rate quickened as she imagined her father deducing why Travis was there.

"I see you brought a guest." His voice was tight, a sure sign that he didn't appreciate the audience.

Yeah, well, she didn't like being ordered to his office as if she was still a child. At that moment, she felt as if a lifetime of holding her true feelings inside was about to erupt.

After a long, assessing look at Travis, her father adjusted the reading glasses on his nose and picked up a file that she suspected held all the store's financials.

"You're spending too much on the store. I've tried to warn you about this before, but you wouldn't listen. We'll be shutting it down by the end of the month and concentrating on selling the farm's products to food processing companies."

Savannah saw red and suddenly realized how often her father had handed down edicts from on high and how much she hated it. She saw movement out of the corner of her eye and sensed Travis was about to jump to her aid. No, this was her fight. She held up her hand, stopping him before he could say anything. Then she took a couple of slow steps closer to her dad and crossed her arms.

"No, we're not. I've put too much work into it, and I have a lot more plans."

"Plans that no doubt cost money. I know you didn't have to worry about money when you were a kid, but it doesn't grow on trees."

Her temper flared. "And I'm not a child anymore, so don't speak to me like I am. I am well aware of what the store's financials are, and they are not out of line with what they should be for a growing small business." That's when she realized something else was behind her father's opposition to the store. Even for him, he was being too harsh about the whole situation. "What's really going on here?"

"I told you."

"No, Dad. You're not telling me something, and if you're determined to take away my dream I deserve to know why."

He tossed down the thick file folder holding her accounting. "Because it reminds me of your mother."

Savannah didn't think he could have said anything that would have stunned her more. She stared at her father, thinking he would surely give her the real reason any moment. "What are you talking about?"

Her dad shifted his gaze toward the window on the opposite side of the room. He remained quiet so long that she thought he wouldn't answer her.

"It was her idea to expand the roadside stand into a store."

Savannah cocked her head to the side. "No, it wasn't. That was my idea."

"It was hers first."

"I don't understand."

"Simple. She suggested it. I said no."

"Why?"

"Because she didn't need to be responsible for something like that. Hell, she couldn't even be responsible enough to stick around to raise her kids."

Savannah jerked back as if she'd been slapped. "So, what? You pushed her away?"

Her dad turned his gaze to her, and this time he was the one who looked hurt. "No, she did that all on her own."

Savannah took a slow, steadying breath, understanding his anger but not how he was taking it out on her. "I'm sorry she hurt you, Dad. But I'm not her. I may have come up with the same idea, may even use her peach pie recipe, but I'm my own woman. And I'm good at my job. You put me in charge of the farm side of the family business. Now you either let me run it, or you hire someone else and I will find a place to live in Dallas and a new job.

I'm done with full-time racing, and I have no interest in the energy business. I'll find my own path."

The stunned expression on her father's face told Savannah she'd finally gotten his full attention, made him realize she wasn't going to be a pushover.

The shock changed to pointed suspicion, however, when he looked at Travis. "You planning to move in with him?"

"If I was, it wouldn't be any of your business. I'm a grown woman, have been for some time now." Savannah took a few steps and leaned one hand against the top of her father's desk. She picked up the carved wooden bull he'd been given when he'd been named North Texas Rancher of the Year. "You know one of the first things I can remember you ever saying about being a good businessman?"

Her father sighed. "Are you about to tell me it was something arrogant?"

"No. You were standing in this room, talking to someone from the company's board of directors. You said that you had to spend money to make money, and that well-planned investments pan out if there's a lot of hard work and passion behind them. I put both of those things into the Peach Pit in spades. So unless you fire me, I'm not giving up on it. In fact, I'm going to make it such a success that you're going to want to claim it was your idea all along."

For what must have been the longest moments in the history of the world, her dad just stared at her. He was probably in shock. She couldn't really believe what she'd just done, either, but she knew this was a huge turning point in her life. Either she was going to be given free rein to grow the store as well as the overall farming operation, or she was going to pack up and start a new life in a different place.

It hit her that doing the latter would make her even more like her mother. Only Savannah wouldn't sever all ties to her family. She glanced at Travis, who leaned against the floor-to-ceiling bookcase next to the door. He gave her a little smile, and she got the feeling he was proud of her. Well, good, because she was proud of herself for standing up to her dad, and not just in a token way to get him to refocus his energies elsewhere.

When she began to think she could no longer stand there in the middle of her father's office bearing the intensity of his scrutiny, he did the oddest thing. He nodded. Then smiled.

"You're right."

"I am?"

He laughed. "Don't lose your nerve now. You just won an argument with your grumpy ass of a father."

Savannah stood up taller. "Good. Because I'm right."

"I believe that's what I said." Her dad picked up the folder and extended it to her. "Go on now. You've evidently got a lot of work to do, especially since you lost a couple of days." He shot Travis a piercing look again, but Travis acted as if it didn't bother him one bit.

Savannah had to hide a smile as she took the folder. "Thank you."

Her dad gave her a quick nod and waved her toward the door. She'd won. She'd really won. Things were definitely looking up. If she made it outside before breaking into a happy dance, she'd be lucky.

She saw the twinkle in Travis's eyes as she neared him. He pushed away from the bookcase to follow her.

"Not you, Travis," her dad said. "I'd like you to stay behind for a few minutes."

She'd evidently thought about celebrating too soon.

What did her dad want with Travis? She spun back around. "Dad—"

Travis caught her gaze and winked at her. "It's okay."

As she hesitantly stepped through the doorway, she wished she could be as certain.

Chapter Thirteen

Travis waited until Savannah had closed the door before he turned back toward her father, wiping any emotion off his face.

"I hear you've been coming around the ranch a lot lately."

Travis didn't say anything in response, forcing Brock to get to his point.

"Why have you come back into Savannah's life?"

Brock Baron was used to being able to rattle people, but Travis wasn't easily intimidated. Once you'd survived boot camp and nearly getting blown up on a daily basis, facing down an overprotective father was a piece of cake.

"You know we ran into each other at the rodeo in Mineral Wells."

"I appreciate you taking her to the hospital, but what about since then? Our ranch isn't exactly on your commute to work."

Travis wasn't the least bit surprised that Brock not only knew where he worked but where he lived. "No, but it's worth the drive."

"Worth the drive to Galveston?"

"Yes, sir."

"So it's more than rekindling an old friendship?"

The intensity in Brock's eyes had probably made teenage boys wither before him and reconsider asking out any of the Baron girls. Travis resisted the irrational urge to laugh.

"Yes, sir, it is."

"Any kind of professional relationship?"

Travis rested his hands on his hips. "I don't discuss my clients. So if there were a professional relationship, I wouldn't tell you."

Brock tensed. Even at his age and with his injured leg, he looked like a ticked-off bull ready to charge. But the longer he stared at Travis, with him staring right back, the more Brock's expression changed to one of grudging respect.

Sensing that Brock's line of questioning had run its course, Travis turned and headed for the door.

"You better be good to my girl," Brock said behind him. The way he said it, Travis had no doubt that, broken leg or not, Brock would find a way to take a pound of flesh out of him if he hurt Savannah in any way.

Travis halfway turned toward Brock. "That you don't have to worry about."

As he left the room, he fully realized that he'd fallen deeply in love with Savannah and would do anything in his power to make her happy.

SAVANNAH COULDN'T KEEP STILL. Instead, she paced the walkway that led to her father's front door.

"You're going to dig a trench to China."

Savannah looked up to see Julieta, who was more a friend than stepmother because of the slim difference in their ages. "Oh, hey."

"What has you so agitated? Did your father say something to upset you?"

"No. Well, yeah, but I handled it."

"But…?"

Savannah gestured toward the front door. "I think he's giving Travis the third degree."

Julieta smiled. "That happens when a man sees another man making a move on his daughter."

Savannah shook her head. "Making a move? Really? As I told Dad, I'm a grown woman."

"Yes, but you'll always be his little girl, same as Lizzie and Carly." Julieta looked toward the house. "So, do you love him?"

Savannah let the question sit there for a few seconds while she thought over everything that had happened between her and Travis in such a short time. He'd taken care of her on more than one occasion, was determined to find her mother for her and was a rock when she needed it. Not to mention he made her feel beautiful, feminine but also strong and able to do anything. Then there was the incredible sex….

"Yes, I do."

Julieta moved closer and took Savannah's hands in hers. "Then you grab onto him and hang on as if your life depends on it. If necessary, I'll rein in your dad."

Savannah smiled. "Thank you."

Julieta pulled Savannah close for a hug. "I'm happy for you."

The front door opened, causing Savannah to quickly pull away from Julieta to face Travis.

"See, he survived the lion's den," Julieta said under her breath before heading up the stone pathway toward the house.

Savannah watched as the two of them greeted each other in passing before she met Travis's eyes. "So, what did he want?"

"He wanted to know my intentions toward his daughter."

"And?"

"I told him I intended to throw you over my shoulder, carry you home and make love to you all night long."

Savannah's mouth dropped open before she swatted him. "Be serious."

"Why? Teasing you is so much more fun."

"Travis."

He pulled her into his arms. "He wanted to know if we were more than friends."

"What did you tell him?"

"That we are more." He dropped his mouth to hers and kissed her, softly, sweetly. "Way more."

Her heart gave an excited thump. The words "I love you" almost slipped from her mouth. But this wasn't where she wanted to tell him, nor the time. Though the truth of it sang within her, she wanted to make sure she wasn't facing cancer before she told him. If she was…she didn't want to think of letting him go, but he'd already been through too much.

Travis moved his mouth next to her ear and said, "Though I think taking you home and making love to you all night isn't a bad idea."

No, not a bad idea at all.

They barely made it up to her apartment before they started ripping off clothes. Thankfully, Carly had closed up the store and gone home.

After they'd both found their release and lay curled around each other in her bed, the need to tell him that she loved him nearly bubbled out. But she couldn't be that selfish. If she got good news, then she'd have plenty of time to tell him how he'd captured her heart. She only hoped he felt the same. He seemed to, and that was enough for now.

They slept for a while, kissed some more, until finally

Travis propped himself up on one elbow. He caressed her cheek, and she wondered how she'd ever been satisfied with her life without him in it. She could be independent and self-confident and still want the joy of being in love, of being loved. She realized there was room in her busy life for this wonderful man, more than enough room.

"I don't want to leave, but I have a client meeting early in the morning."

"It's okay. I've sort of monopolized your weekend."

He leaned toward her. "You didn't hear me complaining, did you?"

Before she could answer, he dropped another kiss on her lips.

While he showered, she unpacked and tossed her dirty clothes into the laundry. She heard her phone beep just as she wandered into the living room. Noticing she had a new message, she punched in the code for her voice mail.

"This is Dr. Fisher's office. We have your test results if you'll call at your earliest convenience."

Travis opened the bathroom door and walked out as she pulled the phone away from her ear, her hand shaking. If they called her on a Sunday, that couldn't be good. But when she noticed the time of the call, it was Friday afternoon.

"Savannah?"

She turned toward the concern in his voice. "My test results are in, have been since Friday afternoon." She held up the phone. "But for some reason the message just dumped onto my phone."

He stepped closer. "What did they say?"

"Just that they were in and to call them." How was she supposed to sleep tonight, waiting for the office to open in the morning?

For several long moments, Travis said nothing. She

imagined him kicking himself for getting involved with someone who could be staring down a cancer diagnosis. But then he pulled her to him.

"I'll stay and go with you in the morning." His voice sounded strained despite his obvious effort to hide it.

"No, you've got work to do."

"Work can wait."

She pulled away from him. "No, please. You have to make a living. I'll be okay. I feel great, so it's probably nothing."

And if it wasn't, she didn't want to see the look on his face when he found out.

TRAVIS FINISHED UP his early-morning meeting and escorted out the couple who had just hired him to investigate whether any of the employees of their company were embezzling. When he stepped into the waiting area next to Blossom's desk, he froze. He stared into the eyes of Irene Crouch. He hadn't seen her since the day her son, David, had been sentenced to life in prison for killing Corinne.

"Travis, this is—"

"I know who she is."

Blossom startled at his abrupt interruption. He wanted to turn around, walk into his office and slam the door. He did not need to be reminded of Corinne's death today of all days. Damn it, he should be at Savannah's side.

Or was this reminder of the hell and pain he'd gone through coming as a warning for him to not get any closer to Savannah?

Well, it was too late for that. He'd already fallen head over heels in love with her.

Irene Crouch stood and walked toward him slowly.

"Mr. Shepard, I know I'm probably the last person you want to see."

"No, that would be your son." He knew he was being harsh, that Mrs. Crouch was no more responsible for Corinne's death than Blossom was, but just thinking about David Crouch made him want to choke the life from the man.

Mrs. Crouch lowered her head and took a shaky breath before lifting her gaze to his again. There were tears in her eyes. "I'm sorry to bother you, but I only ask for a few minutes of your time."

Travis took a moment to forcibly set aside his anger before nodding. He looked at Blossom. "I'll be back in a while."

Blossom, normally so bubbly and full of life, simply nodded that she'd heard.

Wondering what in the world could have brought Mrs. Crouch to his office, he motioned toward the glass door that led into the elevator lobby. "Let's go for a walk."

Neither of them spoke until they'd crossed the street to the park that was crisscrossed with paths. Travis led the way down the central path until they reached a bench next to a fountain. Mrs. Crouch sank down onto the wooden bench as if her legs could no longer support her.

"It hasn't been released to the press yet, so I wanted to see you before it was," she said. She swallowed visibly. "David died early this morning. He…he took his own life."

Shock slammed into Travis, followed by anger. Crouch was supposed to suffer for the rest of his life, trapped like the caged animal he was. Travis felt sucker punched again. First he'd been robbed of his wife, now justice.

Mrs. Crouch reached into her purse and retrieved an

envelope, which she then extended to him. "He told me that if he died in prison before I was gone, that I was to give this to you."

"I don't want whatever that is."

"Please," she said. "He told me not to read it, but I did. I know you were very angry with him, and you had every right to be. And he knew that."

"Nothing in that letter can bring Corinne back." A wave of pain that felt as raw as the day he'd laid Corinne to rest twisted his insides.

"No, it can't. I know you loved her. But David was my only son, and I loved him. He did a horrible thing, but when I looked at him I still saw the little boy who used to curl up in my arms and watch cartoons." Her voice broke, and a tear escaped and ran down her cheek. "I know that it's a lot of me to ask, but please read the letter. If not for David, then for me. For the boy he once was."

Damn if his heart didn't ache for her. He remembered how she'd cried at David's sentencing, how she hadn't even been able to walk from the courtroom under her own power. He'd been so full of hatred and rage then that he hadn't cared. But he did now. Mrs. Crouch was as much a victim as he was. They'd both lost someone that they loved.

Mrs. Crouch, a single mother, had just lost her only child. As bad as it had been to lose Corinne, he couldn't imagine what pain must come from the loss of a child.

He reached over and took the letter. Then, surprising himself, he wrapped his hand around Mrs. Crouch's. "I'm sorry for your loss."

She pressed her lips together and placed her other hand on his. Then she gave him a sad smile before getting to her feet and walking away. She looked so alone that it broke his heart.

He watched her until she reached her car, afraid she might collapse. When she drove away, he looked at the plain envelope in his hand. He wanted to rip it to pieces or simply throw it in the nearest trash can. But he'd promised a grieving mother he'd read it. With anger making it hard not to crumple the envelope, he opened it and pulled out the letter.

Mr. Shepard,
I have no idea if you will read this letter, but I hope you will. Even if you don't, I need to write it. I know I can't say anything that will take away your pain and your anger toward me, and I don't deserve your forgiveness so I won't ask for it. But I want you to know that I am sorry. Very, very sorry. If I could give my life to bring back your wife, I would in a heartbeat. I think about her every day.

Travis had to stop reading and look away from the letter. In that moment, he hated David Crouch more than he ever had. How dare he say he'd give his life for Corinne's. He should have thought about that before he pulled the trigger. Travis's hand shook with the effort to not crush the letter in his fist, imagining it was Crouch's throat. It was exactly what he should do, but for some reason he found his gaze returning to the words written on the paper.

I wish I could take that moment back. I wish I'd never done drugs. I wish I hadn't hurt my mama. I wish so many things that I can't change now. I wish I could do something to make up for what I did. I ruined my life and so many others. Some days I think the guilt will kill me, and some days I hope that it will. It's what I deserve. I hope that some-

how you have found happiness again. If not, I hope
that you do.
David Crouch

Travis sat on the bench staring at David Crouch's name,
the old anger and hatred threatening to consume him.

He looked up and across the park at a young mother
teaching her little boy to ride a tiny bicycle with train-
ing wheels. He couldn't help but wonder if Mrs. Crouch
had done that with David when he'd been young, before
the temptation of drugs had lured him down the wrong
path. If he'd taken a different fork in the road, what kind
of life might he have had? Would he be happily married
now with children of his own? Travis imagined a bright
smile on Mrs. Crouch's face as she was surrounded by
grandchildren instead of the despair she now felt to her
very core.

Would he and Corinne have had children by now? He'd
never know because of David Crouch.

After several long minutes, he stood but didn't return
to the office. Instead, he turned in the opposite direction
and started walking as his stomach turned.

He knew he should call Savannah, but the idea of her
getting bad news hit him in the gut so hard that he couldn't
dial the number. Even if the news was good, would he ever
be able to not worry about her? That he might lose her?

He was a fool for getting so deeply involved with her,
for allowing himself to fall for her. He'd ignored all the
warning signs.

God, he loved her. And that was why he had to stay
away. All he'd had to do was stare into the face of Mrs.
Crouch's grief to remember the feeling of being carved

up inside. To face that again with Savannah— Just the thought was enough to make him wish his ability to fall in love had died with Corinne.

Chapter Fourteen

Savannah stared at her phone, desperate to call Dr. Fisher's office for her test results but also afraid of what she might say. She'd gotten halfway through dialing the number twice only to hang up. She wanted to be strong, but she couldn't help wishing Travis was beside her.

Finally, she took a deep breath and forced herself to dial all the numbers. With her heart threatening to beat itself to death, she listened as the phone rang once, twice.

"Dr. Fisher's office."

"Um, this is Savannah Baron. I had a message that my biopsy results were in."

"Just a moment and I'll connect you with her nurse."

More interminable moments passed as she listened to dreadful elevator-style music. Couldn't they at least play something soothing, like one of those nature recordings of mountain streams or ocean waves?

That image sent her thoughts right back to the weekend in Galveston. Would she ever experience anything that wonderful again? Or had it been her one hurrah before being plunged into hell?

"This is Becky," someone said in her ear, startling her. After a moment, she remembered the cheerful Becky from the day she'd gone to see Dr. Fisher.

Savannah repeated why she was calling.

"Let me look up your records."

Savannah wanted to scream as she listened to Becky typing.

"Here it is. Your biopsy came back negative."

Her heart skipped a beat. "Negative?" Was negative good or bad? "What does that mean?"

"You don't have cancer. And it's not a precancerous lump, either."

"So, I'm healthy?"

"As far as this goes, yes."

Savannah couldn't believe it. She realized she'd prepared herself so much for bad news that it was exactly what she'd been expecting. Realizing she should say something, she finally managed a thank-you before ending the call. Then she sat on the side of her bed staring out the window that revealed another bright, sunny day. It was as if Mother Nature had known she would get good news and given her a beautiful day to celebrate.

A rush of excitement and intense happiness consumed her, and she jumped up as she called Travis. When he didn't answer his cell, she figured he must still be in the meeting. So she dialed his office, intending to leave him a message to call her as soon as he was free.

"Shepard Investigations. How can I help you?"

"Yes, is Travis free?"

"No, can I take a message?"

"Yeah, have him call Savannah as soon as he gets out of his meeting."

Hesitation on the other end of the line caused an odd tingle of worry to pop to life inside Savannah.

"He's out of the office for the rest of the day, but I'll tell him if I hear from him."

Out all day? He hadn't mentioned that. Had something

come up? Did it have to do with the search for her mother? "Oh, okay. Thanks."

When she hung up, she tried his cell again only to get voice mail. She didn't want to leave a message with the news. This was something she wanted to tell him herself. She paced through her apartment, her phone in hand, willing it to ring. But ten minutes went by, then fifteen, and twenty. He knew she was getting the news about her diagnosis this morning. He'd even offered to be with her when she got it. But once he'd gone home alone, had he changed his mind? Had the thought of her having cancer scared him away?

She didn't want to think that, but hadn't she already determined she would push him away if the news had been bad to save him from further pain? Even so, she couldn't deny how it hurt that he hadn't checked with her.

She wiped at sudden tears. Damn it, she wasn't this woman. She'd just gotten the best news of her life, and here she was crying. After washing and drying her face, she went downstairs to put some of her plans for the Peach Pit into action.

By midafternoon, she and Gina had both the peach wedding cake and an order for twenty peach and pecan pies prepared. After the bride-to-be picked up her cake, Gina loaded up the pies for delivery on her way home.

Left alone, Savannah sank onto a chair next to the front window and looked at her phone for what had to be the eight hundredth time. Still no message from Travis. Her heart ached more than she would have ever thought possible.

Trying to push away her hurt, she refocused on the plans for the peach festival. She'd been calling people all day, setting up various vendor booths, a sketch artist to do caricatures, and Amos's to provide barbecue. A nearby rancher who raised miniature horses would bring several for little kids to ride. Her brothers had agreed to man the hayrides, and Carly was in charge of the pumpkin-carving contest.

The front door opened and, speak of the devil, in came Carly. She took one look at Savannah, and her smile fell away.

"What's wrong?"

"Nothing."

"Bull." Carly plopped down in the chair on the other side of the small table. "You're planning this big event and you look as if someone ran over your dog."

"I don't have a dog."

"Smart-ass, you know what I mean. Spill. Wait, did you hear from the doctor?"

Savannah nodded. "Yeah, I'm fine. It's not cancer."

"That's awesome! When did you find out?"

"This morning."

"And you didn't tell me? What the hell?"

Savannah looked out the window, as if that would make Travis appear. "I'm sorry. I've just been so preoccupied today."

"Too preoccupied to tell me that I don't have to worry about you anymore?"

She shifted her attention back to Carly. "I didn't mean to make you worry."

"I know you didn't. So if you got good medical news and Dad is off your back about the store, this has to do with Travis, doesn't it? You two didn't break up, did you?"

"No. I mean, I don't know. I just haven't been able to get in touch with him today."

"Maybe he's busy on a case."

Savannah sighed. "He knew I was getting the news today." She explained about the voice mail she'd received before he left the night before. "I think maybe it spooked him more than he wanted to admit. I can't blame him for not wanting to go through again what he did when Corinne was killed."

"But this isn't the same thing, even if it had been cancer."

"Loss does strange things to people."

"Yeah, well, I'm going to do butt-kicking things to a certain person if he abandoned you right when you needed him most."

Savannah reached across the table and placed her hand on Carly's. "No. Thank you for your support, but we'll work this out. Or we won't."

She tried not to jump to conclusions. But as the hours passed with no word from Travis, her heart sank more and more. While part of her truly did understand why he would want to protect himself, she couldn't help the anger that started to build within her. Why had he led her to believe he cared only to leave? Especially when he knew how badly it had hurt her when her mother did the same thing.

If Travis and she really were over, thank God she still had the Peach Pit. Because single-minded focus was how she'd handled her mother leaving, even if she hadn't realized it at the time. From that point, her life had revolved around getting good grades and being a champion barrel racer. She'd needed to be good enough that no one would ever leave her again.

Fat lot of good that had done her.

TRAVIS SEARCHED THROUGH all the files on his desk, growing more frustrated by the second. "Blossom, where's the Brinkman case file?"

"In your filing cabinet," she called back.

"No, it's not. I just looked."

A moment later, Blossom stalked into his office, went to the filing cabinet and pulled out a file. She spun and crossed to his desk, then shoved the file at him.

When he met her gaze, he noticed her tight expression. "What's with you?"

"My boss has been an ass the past week."

Travis paused as he grabbed the folder. "No, I haven't."

She lifted a brow. "Yes, you have. I work here because it's interesting and you're a good boss. I've had jerk bosses before, so I don't need another one."

Travis let the file folder drop to his desk and sank into his chair. "Have I really been that bad?"

He'd been alternating between hating David Crouch and himself for days, but he hadn't realized he'd been taking it out on Blossom.

"Yes, you have." Blossom leaned against the edge of his desk. "I understand that Mrs. Crouch's visit threw you for a loop, but that's not all that's bothering you."

"So you're a mind reader now?"

"You're not that hard to read. You miss Savannah, and for some reason you've cut off ties to her."

"I never said that."

"Again, not that hard to read."

Travis sighed. "I thought I could handle being in a relationship again, but seeing Mrs. Crouch showed me I'm not."

"Because you're still in love with Corinne?"

He thought about that question for a moment before shaking his head. "I can't go through losing someone like that again."

"So you're going to avoid women for the rest of your life?"

"I don't know. Maybe."

"Not to be insensitive, but that's the dumbest thing I've ever heard."

Travis was used to Blossom speaking her mind, but she'd never been cruel.

"Don't look at me that way," she said. "I'm not saying that the fear of being hurt is invalid. We all live with that every day. It's part of our genetic code or something. But you know what? We go out and live our lives anyway. And if you're not going to fully live yours, that's not fair to Corinne."

"What the hell is that supposed to mean?"

"Because she didn't get to live her life to its full potential. You do."

Her words hit him straight in the heart.

"And what about Savannah? She's experienced hurt and betrayal before. How do you think she's feeling right now that you dropped off the radar?"

"I didn't mean to hurt her," he said.

"Well, I'm going to bet you did. And I don't blame her if she's ticked off at you." Blossom placed her hand atop his. "You and Corinne got a really raw deal, no doubt about it. But if you don't grab every chance at happiness that life has to offer and enjoy it despite the fear, you might as well have died that day, too."

She stood and headed toward the door.

"Blossom?"

He stared at her for a moment, not knowing what to say.

"Are you about to fire me? I'm okay with that because all that needed to be said, and most people are chicken to hand out the tough love."

Part of him was angry that she was forcing him to face his biggest fear, losing someone else he loved. But as he stared at the absolute certainty in her expression, he knew she was right. "Thank you."

"You're welcome. Does that mean I still have a job?"

He managed a smile. "Yes. I'm never letting you go."

"Ha! I let you keep me." With that she headed back to her desk and the ringing phone.

Could he do it? Let go of the anger and fear that had ruled him for so long?

Travis opened the desk drawer where he'd stashed David Crouch's letter. He'd nearly burned it at least a dozen times, but something had stopped him. He looked down at the letter again, rereading every word. He hated to admit it, but he felt the truth of the apology. David Crouch truly had been sorry, had been haunted by what he'd done, so much so that he'd taken his own life.

The tragedy of the entire situation made Blossom's words burn brighter. Suddenly, Travis wanted to grab onto life with both hands and not let go, to live it to the absolute fullest. He might not have been able to prevent Corinne's death, but he could live a life that honored her. But would fate allow that? Or had his hate doomed him to nothing but more pain? He almost called Savannah, but that would have to wait a little longer. He had something else to do first.

As THE DAYS PASSED, Savannah continued working on the peach festival and even fleshed out some of the other ideas from the master list she and Travis had drafted that night at Amos's. She investigated all the ins and outs for setting up an online store, thinking about how it could be a big moneymaker during the holidays. When she was tired of sitting, she went back to the kitchen and set about preparing a new peach tart recipe. She had to stay busy or she would dissolve into tears as she had more than once over the past week. A week without word of any kind from Travis.

It was almost dark when someone knocked on the front door, startling her. When she looked up and saw that it was Travis, her heart leaped. She wanted to race to the door and into his arms, but another part of her wanted to ignore him. She compromised and forced herself to walk slowly toward the door.

"Hello," she said when she opened the door, trying to keep the frost out of her voice.

"I'm sorry."

"For?" She wasn't going to make this easy on him.

"Not calling, disappearing."

"It got the point across." She thought she saw him wince, and it gave her a momentary flash of pleasure.

"You have every right to be angry, but I'm here to beg your forgiveness. I got scared, and I handled it in the worst possible way." He hesitated, took a breath. "What did the doctor say?"

She tamped down the sudden burst of anger. He should have asked that question days ago. She'd wanted to celebrate the good news with him, but he'd obviously let his past dictate his present.

"I'm fine. It's not cancer."

His smile and obvious happiness was immediate, and he took a step toward her as if he might pull her into his arms. Instinctively, she backed away from him. The smile fell from his lips.

"I would take back my actions if I could," he said.

She could see in his eyes that he was telling the truth, and she couldn't help softening the slightest bit.

"I tried to convince myself that I understood if you needed to pull away. You shouldn't have to go through losing someone again like you did with Corinne. But I'm evidently not that strong. I needed you, and you weren't there. It was as if every inkling that you cared for me went out like a light. It hurt, a lot."

Travis slowly closed the distance between them and took her hand in his. "You're right that Corinne is the reason I didn't call, but it's not what you think." He looked down at her hand and ran his thumb across her skin. "I had a surprise visitor at the office the day you got your news. David Crouch's mother."

The shock of that revelation pushed aside Savannah's hurt. "Why did she come see you?"

"He had written a letter to me, to be delivered by her should he die."

"So, he…"

"He killed himself. I'm surprised you haven't seen it on the news."

"I've had other things on my mind."

Travis lowered his gaze, and she felt the guilt coursing through him. It brought her closer to forgiving him.

"I couldn't believe she was there to see me only hours after he died."

Savannah didn't know the woman, but she ached for her. No matter what David had done, he was still her son.

More of her anger slipped away when she thought about all the old pain seeing Mrs. Crouch must have caused Travis. "Are you okay?"

He lifted his gaze to hers and looked as if he thought it was a miracle she would ask. "Yeah, for the first time in years."

"Because he's dead?" She would understand if he said yes, but it still felt harsh, at odds with the kindness she knew was very much a part of who Travis was, the last week of her hurt feelings aside.

Travis entwined his fingers with hers. "No, which is the biggest surprise of all. I didn't want to read the letter, but I did. It was an apology. At first, it made me so angry. I know this sounds stupid, but I thought maybe it was a sign that I shouldn't open myself up to that kind of pain again. When I thought of losing you the way I did Corinne...I ran. I'm not proud of it."

"Then why are you here now?"

"Because I have a good friend who told me what an idiot I was being." He lifted his hand and caressed her cheek. "And because this past week without you, I haven't been able to stop thinking about you, missing you, no matter how hard I tried."

Despite how he'd hurt her, Savannah's heart sang at his words.

"I knew I had to let go of the past to be fair to you. I made myself read Crouch's letter again. I'd hated him for so long that I didn't want to believe anything he said, but it was the oddest thing. I..." He shook his head slowly. "I could feel the truth of it, how he would have honestly given his life to bring Corinne back. I ended up walking around probably half of downtown Dallas just thinking."

He looked up and met her gaze. "It was the strangest feeling, as if the longer I walked the more of the anger and pain I left like a trail behind me. By the time I rounded back to the office, it was as if a weight I hadn't even known was there wasn't anymore."

Travis ran the backs of his fingers across her cheek. "There was all this new space within me, and I want to fill it with you."

Her heart, which had been heavy all day, filled to bursting. "I was so afraid that what we'd shared was over."

"I'm sorry I made you feel that way." He leaned forward and planted a light kiss on her mouth. "Will you go for a walk with me?"

"Yes."

Travis placed her hand in the crook of his arm and led her outside and toward the orchard. The light of the full moon made it bright enough to see without the benefit of flashlights as they strolled between two rows of peach trees. Savannah told him about the festival she was planning, the mail-order business, all her grand ideas. Her love for him grew with every step as he not only said everything sounded great but also tossed in even more ways to make the Peach Pit everything she wanted it to be.

They'd gone a good distance when Travis finally stopped and turned toward her.

"During all my walking today, I wasn't just thinking. I had another purpose."

"You needed some exercise? I can think of something better than walking around Dallas."

"I can, too, and I'm hoping we get around to that." He reached into his pocket and pulled out something. "For many years to come."

When he lowered himself to one knee in front of her and lifted his hand, a ring glinted in the moonlight. She gasped.

"Savannah Baron, I never thought I'd love someone again, but you started proving me wrong that night I saw you at the rodeo. Since then, I've loved you more every time I've been with you, even when that scared me half to death. I want to be with you the rest of my life, if you'll have me." He paused, smiling. "Will you marry me?"

All the hurt and doubt slid away as she heard the deep sincerity in his words.

"Yes. Oh, my God, yes!"

She could barely stand still as Travis slipped the ring onto her finger. "I didn't get you a diamond. I know you can't tell out here now, but it's an orange sapphire. It reminded me of these peaches you love so much."

"It's perfect," she said, not needing to see the color to know that she would treasure it for the rest of her days. "You're perfect. At least you would be if you'd get up here and kiss me."

Travis laughed and got to his feet. "Yes, ma'am."

When he kissed her this time, it wasn't a soft touching of lips. He pulled her close and kissed her as if they were outlawing kisses at the stroke of midnight. She had no idea how much time passed before they came up for air. But when they did, something occurred to her.

"You bought this ring before you knew my diagnosis."

"Yes, I did. I realized that it didn't matter if we had months or decades—I wanted to spend them with you as my wife."

She'd never been touched by something so deeply in her life. "I love you, more than I ever imagined I could love someone."

"Good." He scooped her up into his arms, making her squeal, and started retracing their steps. "Because I don't think I've had enough exercise today."

She giggled. "I could stand to work off a couple of peach pastries."

"Honey, by the time this night is over, you're going to need a lot more than a couple of pastries to recover."

"Then it's a good thing I have an entire orchard full of peaches."

Maybe someday they'd find her mother, but for now Savannah couldn't ask for anything more. She was healthy, loved her job and was so in love with the man carrying her that she didn't think words could express it. And thanks to the most unexpected source, Travis was finally free to truly love her back.

Despite what he'd done, Savannah sent out a silent

thank-you to David Crouch. She hoped he and Corinne were both at peace.

When they arrived back at the Peach Pit, Travis set her on her feet on the front steps. When he looked at her, there was such love in his eyes that it took her breath away.

"What are you thinking?" she asked.

"That I wish I could go back and tell my dorky teenage self not to worry, that I would someday get the girl. And she was worth the wait."

She smiled. "I already said yes, you know."

"Yes, you did. And I'm going to hold you to it."

She took his hand and started backing toward the door. "What do you say we go seal the deal?"

"Only if you tell me you need lots of convincing."

"Loads."

He gave her a wicked grin. "Good answer."

Chapter Fifteen

Travis poured himself a cup of coffee and walked as quietly as he could down the center aisle of the Peach Pit and out the front door. Savannah had a big day ahead of her, one she'd worked hard to pull together in a short amount of time, and he wanted to let her sleep a little longer. Plus, he wanted some private minutes to think, to make a decision regarding an idea he'd been mulling for the past few days.

He sank onto the top porch step and took a drink of his coffee. Only the barest hint of daylight was touching the eastern horizon, hardly visible through the layer of fog that blanketed the ranch. He inhaled a deep breath and marveled at the quiet. Even at this hour, Dallas wouldn't be without some sort of noise. He'd never really thought about it before or let it bother him, but he had to admit that the hush and solitude that surrounded him now was peaceful.

Peace was something he'd convinced himself he'd never truly have in the aftermath of Corinne's death, but the events of the past few weeks had proven otherwise. Love had replaced pain in his heart. Existing had given way to truly living. And most surprising of all, forgiveness had taken up residence where hatred and anger had made camp for too long. He felt like a different man now than he had the night of that rodeo in Mineral Wells. A better man.

Somewhere out in the darkness, a songbird began to herald the new day. He wasn't a morning person by nature, but even he had to admit there was an allure to this time of day. A person could truly think when not being bombarded by noise from every direction.

He looked up toward the sky, at the blanket of stars that wouldn't be visible for much longer. He imagined Corinne looking down at him and smiling. Since he'd proposed to Savannah two weeks ago, the tie he had to Corinne had changed. It would never go away, and he'd always love her. But it felt as if she'd given her approval. He couldn't explain why he felt that way, but he figured there would always be things he couldn't explain.

Like how his thoughts had gone to Irene Crouch a lot lately. When he'd seen a news segment showing the media camped out in front of her house after the details of David's death were released, anger had risen up in him again. But this time it wasn't at her or her son, but at the people who wouldn't leave her alone. By all accounts, she'd done the best she could raising her son by herself. But he'd gone down a bad path, and she'd lost him forever because of it. He hated the idea of her sitting inside her house, mourning alone, unable to step outside without a camera and microphone being shoved in her face. He knew what that felt like, and it wasn't right.

And he doubted he could explain it to anyone, but it also didn't feel right that she was suffering while he was so incredibly happy. But if anyone could understand, he'd bet it was Savannah.

His thoughts of the woman he loved turned into the real thing when she opened the door behind him. When he glanced over his shoulder, he noticed that Savannah carried her own coffee mug.

"Did I wake you?" he asked.

"Not at all." She came to sit beside him. "Though I think my early morning tendencies are beginning to rub off on you."

He leaned over and planted a soft kiss on her lips. "I can think of worse things."

She smiled. "This from the man who not so long ago could only grunt responses at daybreak."

"What can I say? Early mornings are a lot better when I wake up next to you."

"If only your army buddies knew what kind of sweet talker you are. I wonder what Evan would say."

"You, Miss Baron, are ornery."

"Who, me? I'm an angel." She held both hands above her head, forming her fingers into a halo.

He wrapped an arm around her waist and tugged her close. "You have the world fooled, but not me."

This time, his kiss held a lot more heat and lasted considerably longer. Savannah kissed him back with an enthusiasm that made every nerve in his body hum before she pulled away.

"I think we'd better cool it," she said. "I have way too much to do this morning to be tempted by my fiancé."

"Does that mean you're kicking me out?"

"I'm sure you can find something to do."

He glanced down at his half-consumed cup of coffee. "Actually, I do have somewhere I need to go."

Savannah looked at him with a fleeting moment of curiosity before nodding as if she knew what had been distracting him the past few days. She smiled and leaned over to plant a soft kiss on his cheek.

"You're a good man, Travis Shepard."

"Good enough to marry?"

"Yep. Go, do what you need to. I'll see you later."

After she went inside, he took a few more minutes to finish his coffee and watch as night gave way to day. As he took his last swig, however, he rose to his feet. The peach festival would be getting under way midmorning, and he fully intended to be back to the ranch to see the fruition of Savannah's hard work.

He expected anxiety to twist his gut as he drove toward Dallas and then through the series of streets that brought him to a neighborhood that had seen better, more prosperous times. But it didn't, and a voice in his head told him it was because this was the right thing to do. Though the streets weren't filled with crack houses or shot up like the more dangerous areas of the city, the small houses could use new coats of paint that their owners likely couldn't afford.

When he reached a dingy white house on the corner that was so small it could fit in Savannah's apartment, he pulled over next to the sidewalk and parked. His SUV looked out of place amongst vehicles that had rolled off the assembly line when Ronald Reagan was president.

He scanned the street but only saw a couple of people, a woman in a robe placing envelopes in her mailbox and an elderly man sitting on his porch watching the world go by. Thankfully, the media had evidently moved on to someone else's tragedy and vacated the area.

With a quick, deep breath, he got out of the vehicle and took the short, cracked concrete walkway up to Irene Crouch's porch. When he knocked, at first he didn't hear anything. He wondered if she'd stopped answering the door. Maybe she'd had to stop all those years ago when David had made his fatal mistake.

He'd raised his hand to knock again when the white

sheer curtain hanging over the window to his right was pulled aside. It almost immediately dropped back into place, followed a moment later by the front door opening.

"Mr. Shepard, I didn't expect to see you. Can I help you?"

"I just wanted to see how you were doing."

He doubted she could have looked more shocked if he'd told her she'd won a fortune.

"I'm fine," she finally said.

She'd lowered her eyes as she said it, but not before he'd seen the truth there.

"Do you have any plans for today?"

When she met his eyes, her face was filled with confusion. "No. I…I don't go out much other than to work and the grocery store."

He pulled one of the flyers for the festival from his pocket and extended it to her. "I'd like to invite you to this. It's being held about an hour from here, on my fiancée's family ranch."

"You're getting married again?"

"Yes, ma'am. You actually helped me come to that decision."

"Me?"

He nodded. "The day you came to see me, what you said and…David's letter made me realize that time is precious. There was no going back to undo anything that was done, but I could move forward."

Irene pressed her lips together and blinked several times. She took the paper he held and unfolded it. She skimmed the list of activities that would fill the day and hopefully draw a big crowd.

"It sounds like a nice event, but I don't think it's a good idea for me to go."

Travis didn't even think about it before he reached forward and took Irene's hands in his. She didn't look up at him, but she did take a shaky breath and sniff.

"I hope you reconsider." He didn't push her. Only she would know when she'd be ready to come out and face the world again, take that first step toward living.

Irene didn't speak, and he suspected she probably couldn't in that moment. When she gave him a slight nod instead, he released her hands and retraced his steps to the SUV. Once he was in the driver's seat, he looked back toward the house to find Irene still standing in the doorway looking at the flyer. He could feel her yearning from where he sat, and he truly hoped that she'd find the strength to come out to the ranch, if only for a few minutes.

As he drove back toward the ranch and Savannah, his heart felt lighter. Today was going to be a good day. The best.

SAVANNAH LAUGHED AS she sat atop a stack of hay bales watching Alex and several other kids running through the hay bale maze her brothers had constructed.

"He's going to sleep well tonight," she said to Travis, who'd just brought her a scoop of peach ice cream and sank onto the hay bale next to her.

"I think we probably all will after today."

"If he goes to sleep without demanding I read him no less than five stories, I'm going to push for one of these festivals every weekend," Julieta said from where she stood next to the entrance to the maze.

Savannah made a strangled sound. "As much as I'm loving this, I don't think I'm quite up for that."

Alex came racing out of the maze, all squeals and laughter. Julieta scooped him up and headed for the front porch of the Peach Pit, where Savannah's dad sat in his wheelchair observing all the activity going on around him like a king on his throne. She remembered what she'd told her dad about making the Peach Pit so successful that he'd wish it had been his idea all along. By the look on his face, she thought maybe she'd taken at least a few steps toward that goal.

Her heart swelled at how her family had come together to make the event successful. Carly seemed to be having a great time manning the face painting station even though she kept shooting glances at the crowd, as if she expected to see someone in particular. Jet and Daniel drove the tractors pulling the hay wagons for rides. Jacob was giving roping lessons, and even Lizzie was helping out by manning the cash register in the store. She'd been given strict orders by everyone to stay off her feet, so they'd pulled a stool up to the register. While Lizzie stayed inside out of the heat, her fiancé Chris was staying cool by being repeatedly dumped into the dunking booth tank. Savannah's brothers had even taken several shots at the target, barely giving Chris time to climb out of the water before they sent him right back down.

Travis's arm came around Savannah's waist and pulled her close. "You've done a great job with this."

She looked up into those gorgeous blue eyes of his. "I had a lot of help."

He dropped a quick kiss onto her lips before something drew his attention. Savannah shifted her gaze behind her and saw a woman walking slowly around the edge of the crowd.

"That's her, isn't it?" She looked back at Travis. "Mrs. Crouch."

He nodded. "I hope you don't mind that I invited her."

"Of course not." She lifted her hand to his cheek. "It only makes me love you more."

He squeezed her hand before hopping off their perch and maneuvering through the groups of people toward Irene Crouch. Just when she thought she couldn't love the man who would soon be her husband any more, he proved her wrong. Sometimes she worried that she'd gotten too lucky, that something would happen to take it all away, to leave her feeling empty and alone like she had as a seven-year-old girl wondering if she'd ever see her mother again.

She shook off the thought, determined that this day would bring nothing but joy. After taking the last bite of her ice cream cone, she wiped her hand on a napkin and rejoined the crowd. She talked to neighbors and newcomers alike as she made the rounds, even stopping when she crossed paths with Travis and Mrs. Crouch to tell the older woman that she was glad she could come to the festival.

Irene looked stunned, as if she feared that any moment the crowd would turn on her. But as the afternoon progressed, Savannah caught sight of her a few more times. Once, there was even a hint of a smile on her face as she watched several kids jump around and turn flips inside the bouncy castle. If Irene was thinking of David at that age, Savannah was glad that the memory had brought her a flicker of happiness instead of tears.

When Savannah came near the front of the Peach Pit, she sat on the edge of the porch and smiled at her father. "So, what's the verdict, old man?"

"You do know I'm going to get out of this chair at some point, right?"

She laughed, glad to see her dad in a good mood.

Brock scanned the crowd. "You've proven that you just might be smarter than your daddy."

Pride swelled within her. Though she'd been determined to succeed with or without her father's validation, she couldn't deny it was nice to have.

"Who's that Travis is talking to? I don't recognize her."

Savannah searched the faces spread out in all directions until she spotted Travis handing Irene a plate of barbecue. "Someone who needs a friend."

She didn't explain further, and thankfully her dad didn't ask for more details.

As the sun started heading toward the west, a band that Jet had hired for the evening began setting up. That was her cue. She turned to search for Travis to find him standing right behind her.

"You ready?" he asked.

"More than ready."

He took her hand and led her up the steps at the end of the flatbed trailer where the band was unloading their gear and tuning instruments. Travis led her to the microphone and tapped on it to make sure it was on.

"Hello, everyone," he said. "I'd like to introduce you to the lady who has made all this possible—Savannah Baron."

Savannah's face flushed as she acknowledged the cheers from the crowd. Her heart beating wildly, she stepped up to the microphone. "Good afternoon. I hope everyone is having a great time." After some more clapping and cheers, she continued. "We've got a lot more on tap for this evening, including music and dancing. And don't miss Amos's barbecue plates. He'll ruin you for any other barbecue place in the state of Texas."

Amos doffed his hat in her direction then went back to dishing up food.

"But before we start the music, we've got a special surprise."

Her pulse thumped like a hummingbird's wings. She looked toward the porch of the Peach Pit and saw that all of the members of her family had gathered there. As she spotted Travis's family standing near the dunking booth, he stepped close and took her hand. He squeezed it in that way he had of giving her courage.

"We're going to have a wedding." She looked up at Travis and love filled her to overflowing. "Today, I'm making an honest man out of Travis Shepard and bringing him into this crazy Baron clan."

The cheers this time were a lot louder and more enthusiastic, which only made her smile grow that much wider. Before anyone in her family could rush forward and push for a big, traditional wedding, something she and Travis had decided they didn't want, they looked to the edge of the stage to signal Reverend Tillman. The minister came forward, and she and Travis faced each other, still holding hands.

Though they were surrounded by hundreds of people, several friends, some family and many strangers, everyone faded away except the man in front of her. He was the love of her life, and she felt like the luckiest woman in the world for having found him. What made her heart fill with joy, however, was how he was returning her gaze as if thinking the same about her.

Somehow she made her way through the vows, saying the right thing at the right time. When Reverend Tillman finally said, "I now pronounce you man and wife," she knew that was the single happiest moment of her life.

Travis pulled her close for the kiss but paused right before touching her lips. "I guess you're stuck with me now, Mrs. Shepard."

"I wouldn't have it any other way."

He kissed her then, and she felt it all the way down to the tips of her toes. If she'd thought the cheering earlier was loud, it paled in comparison to what erupted as they kissed. In fact, she was pretty sure that people in downtown Dallas heard the roar.

When the kiss finally ended, she and Travis turned to face the crowd. Her gaze went straight to where her family stood together, nervous to see their reactions.

Every single one of them was smiling and cheering. Even cranky, crusty, large-and-in-charge Brock Baron looked as if he might have a tear in his eye.

The band struck up a lively tune behind them, and Travis pulled her close.

"It's time you dance with me, wife."

She couldn't agree more. Savannah Baron Shepard took center stage and danced with her husband.

* * * * *

Be sure to look for the next book in the
TEXAS RODEO BARONS *miniseries!*
Author Barbara White Daille continues
the Baron family saga with
THE TEXAN'S LITTLE SECRET
available in August 2014 from American Romance!

REQUEST YOUR FREE BOOKS!
2 FREE NOVELS PLUS 2 FREE GIFTS!

HARLEQUIN

American ★ Romance®

LOVE, HOME & HAPPINESS

YES! Please send me 2 FREE Harlequin® American Romance® novels and my 2 FREE gifts (gifts are worth about \$10). After receiving them, if I don't wish to receive any more books, I can return the shipping statement marked "cancel." If I don't cancel, I will receive 4 brand-new novels every month and be billed just \$4.74 per book in the U.S. or \$5.24 per book in Canada. That's a savings of at least 14% off the cover price! It's quite a bargain! Shipping and handling is just 50¢ per book in the U.S. and 75¢ per book in Canada.* I understand that accepting the 2 free books and gifts places me under no obligation to buy anything. I can always return a shipment and cancel at any time. Even if I never buy another book, the two free books and gifts are mine to keep forever.

154/354 HDN F4YN

Name _____ (PLEASE PRINT)

Address _____ Apt. #

City _____ State/Prov. _____ Zip/Postal Code

Signature (if under 18, a parent or guardian must sign)

Mail to the **Harlequin® Reader Service:**
IN U.S.A.: P.O. Box 1867, Buffalo, NY 14240-1867
IN CANADA: P.O. Box 609, Fort Erie, Ontario L2A 5X3

Want to try two free books from another line?
Call 1-800-873-8635 or visit www.ReaderService.com.

* Terms and prices subject to change without notice. Prices do not include applicable taxes. Sales tax applicable in N.Y. Canadian residents will be charged applicable taxes. Offer not valid in Quebec. This offer is limited to one order per household. Not valid for current subscribers to Harlequin American Romance books. All orders subject to credit approval. Credit or debit balances in a customer's account(s) may be offset by any other outstanding balance owed by or to the customer. Please allow 4 to 6 weeks for delivery. Offer available while quantities last.

Your Privacy—The Harlequin® Reader Service is committed to protecting your privacy. Our Privacy Policy is available online at www.ReaderService.com or upon request from the Harlequin Reader Service.

We make a portion of our mailing list available to reputable third parties that offer products we believe may interest you. If you prefer that we not exchange your name with third parties, or if you wish to clarify or modify your communication preferences, please visit us at www.ReaderService.com/consumerschoice or write to us at Harlequin Reader Service Preference Service, P.O. Box 9062, Buffalo, NY 14269. Include your complete name and address.

HAR13R

SPECIAL EXCERPT FROM

 HARLEQUIN

American Romance

*Harlequin American Romance is excited to introduce a
new six-book continuity—* **TEXAS RODEO BARONS!**
Read the following excerpt from
THE TEXAN'S LITTLE SECRET, *where Carly Baron
confronts her past in the form of cowboy Luke Nobel…*

The cowboy standing in the barn doorway started toward
the truck. He wore a battered Stetson, the wide brim
shading most of his face, but no matter how much she tried
to convince herself this was just any old cowhand striding
toward her, she couldn't believe the lie.

He halted within arm's reach of her driver's door, his
eyes seeming to pin her into her seat. "Carly Baron," he
said. "At last."

"Luke." She forced a grin. "Isn't this flattering. Seems
like you were just waiting for the chance to run into me."

"I figured it was bound to happen once Brock said you'd
come home again. But when I never caught sight of you,
I started to wonder if he'd been hitting the pain pills too
hard."

"I'm not home again. I'm just visiting."

"The helpful daughter."

"That's me." She shoved open the door and a double
dose of attitude made her stand straight in front of him.
He stared back without saying a word. Let him look all he
wanted. One touch, though, and she'd deck him.

"It's been a long time."

"And you've come a long way." If he picked up on the

added meaning behind her words, he didn't show it. "I hear you're ranch manager now. Daddy's right-hand man. You finally landed the job you'd always wanted."

He got that message, all right. His jaw hardened. "You think that's what it was all about? I wanted to get to your daddy through you?"

"I said that to you then, and you didn't argue. But it looks like you found a way without me, after all."

"Funny. By now, I would have thought you'd grown up some."

"I expected you'd have grown beyond working for my daddy."

"A man's gotta have a job," he said mildly. "And I guess none of us knows what the future has in store."

"I'm not concerned about the future, only in what's happening today. *And* in making sure not to repeat the past."

"Yeah. Well, what's happening in my world today includes managing this ranch. I'd better get back to it."

"That's what Daddy pays you for," she said.

He touched the brim of his Stetson. "See you around."

Not if I can help it.

Look for THE TEXAN'S LITTLE SECRET
by Barbara White Daille, the first installment in the
TEXAS RODEO BARONS *miniseries.*
Available August 2014
wherever books and ebooks are sold.

American Romance®

He never expected to see her again!

When Mack Cash's mysterious one-night stand shows up at the dude ranch where he works, he is stunned. And just as he suspected during their night together, Beth Richards is no buckle bunny, despite the getup she was wearing. Instead, she's just the kind of woman he's looking for—sexy, sure, but also down-home and whip-smart.

Mack's obvious attraction is just the boost Beth was looking for after a hurtful divorce. She loves the way he looks at her—and sees her. Except for one thing. He wants a family, and Beth can only disappoint him. She's already failed at love once and she can't go through it again. That's why she has to let Mack go….

Look for
TRUE BLUE COWBOY
by MARIN THOMAS

from *The Cash Brothers* miniseries from
Harlequin American Romance.

Available August 2014 wherever books and ebooks are sold.

Also available now from *The Cash Brothers* miniseries by
Marin Thomas:

THE COWBOY NEXT DOOR
TWINS UNDER THE CHRISTMAS TREE
HER SECRET COWBOY
THE COWBOY'S DESTINY

Ameriᴄan Romance®

King and Queen of the Rodeo

Driving to Vegas with the Sexiest Cowboy of the Year is a dream
come true for barrel racing finalist Liz Henson. Now's her
chance to get up close and personal with Connor Bannock, her
secret girlhood crush—even if their families are on the wrong
side of a long-standing feud. It's also her shot at rodeo fame
before she returns to working as a veterinarian, taking care of
the horses she loves.

Look for
A COWBOY'S HEART
by REBECCA WINTERS

from the *Hitting Rocks Cowboys* miniseries
from Harlequin American Romance.

Available August 2014 wherever books and ebooks are sold.

Also available now from the
Hitting Rocks Cowboys miniseries by Rebecca Winters:

IN A COWBOY'S ARMS